# Marriage is Murder

A SUSAN WILES SCHOOLHOUSE / SUGARBURY FALLS
CROSSOVER MYSTERY

by

## Diane Weiner

Copyright © 2022 by Diane Weiner

For information, visit our website at:
www.cozycatpress.com

COZY CAT
PRESS

ISBN: 978-1-952579-43-1
Printed in the United States of America

10 9 8 7 6 5 4 3 2 1

# Chapter 1

Mike snaked the car past Lake Pleasant, through the evergreen-lined road, onto the gravel driveway. "We're here, Susan. Wake up." He'd parked outside a Lincoln-log-like cabin. Two chubby jack-o-lanterns stood sentinel at the entrance.

Retired teacher Susan Wiles stirred in the seat next to her husband. "Are we there yet?"

"Yep. Sugarbury Falls. We made good time. You've been snoring away since we hit the Vermont border."

Susan wiped her bifocals on her sweatshirt. "I don't snore." She pulled down the visor over the glove compartment and checked herself in the mirror.

"Come on. I've been sitting the better part of four hours," said Mike. He popped the trunk while Susan fluffed her blonde-gray hair and dabbed on muted pink lipstick.

A middle-aged couple ran out the front door. Emily Fox, fiftyish with auburn hair and an athletic build, hugged Susan. "I'm so glad you came. We've missed you."

Henry Fox, handsome with slight graying around the temples,

and warm and welcoming as an apple pie in winter, hugged Susan and gave Mike a half-hug, half *'hey bro'* slap on the back. "How was the trip? Did the storm slow you down?"

Mike said, "The rain wasn't too bad. Only passed one accident on the way into town. I expected fall foliage traffic, but was pleasantly surprised."

"If you'd come when St. Edwards had a home football game, it'd be a different story," said Henry.

A three-legged lab had followed Henry to the driveway, tail wagging.

Susan bent down to pet him. "Who's this friendly fellow?" He licked Susan's face.

"That's Spunky, Henry's pride and joy." Emily shivered, having rushed out in a long-sleeved t-shirt sans jacket. "Let's go inside."

A blond teenager met them at the door cradling a black cat in her arms. "Aunt Susan, Uncle Mike!" She gave them each a peck on the cheek. "It's good to see you again."

"Maddy! You're looking so grown-up," said Susan. Maddy had been adopted at the age of fourteen and was now starting her senior year of high school. She hadn't really changed that much in three years, but the comment slipped out of her mouth before she thought it through.

They sat around the wooden table, hand-made by Henry when he first inherited the family cabin. Blue and white checkered placemats were set with dessert plates and matching linen napkins. Susan drank in the aroma of fresh baking.

Mike went into his suitcase and retrieved a bottle of wine. "This is for later."

Emily brought coffee and warm pumpkin bread to the table. They chatted about Maddy's college applications, the new hire at Henry's hospital, and Emily's upcoming true crime book release.

Susan filled them in on their son Evan's wedding plans, and their daughter's pregnancy. And, of course, Susan had a phone full of pictures showing off their granddaughters.

Mike said, "I taught Annalise to ride a bike. No training wheels."

"And her little sister wanted to do the same," said Susan. "Mike convinced Mia training wheels were way cooler than plain old tires."

"I wouldn't have minded putting training wheels on my Jeep while I taught Maddy how to drive," said Henry. Maddy rolled her eyes.

They sat around the table for so long, Susan's bottom felt numb. When Henry suggested a walk, she was the first one up. She pulled a heavy cardigan out of her suitcase and slipped it over her sweatshirt.

"Coming, Maddy?" asked Emily.

"No, I'll stay here with Chester." The cat purred. "See you when you get back."

Henry led them out the kitchen door and onto the wet road. "Sun's out. Things will dry out in a jiffy. Meanwhile, watch for puddles."

When they got near the lake, they ventured off onto a gravel trail. Susan wished she'd worn her rain boots. Her brand new Reeboks wouldn't stay white for long at this rate. The golden sun enhanced the multi-colored mountains and the air smelled of pine trees and wet leaves.

Susan looked up at the vivid blue sky, watched a squirrel scoot across the trail, and took a slow breath. "It's beautiful here." The brisk air chased away remnants of sleepiness from the long trip and the lethargy courtesy of a belly full of pumpkin bread. When they turned the corner, she had a panoramic view of the lake, shimmering in the sunlight.

"The pier is up ahead," said Henry. "Maddy and her friends like to hang out there."

Emily said, "In the summer, they swim here. Of course, now it's too cold."

"When I was a kid and came here to visit my grandparents," said Henry, "we'd go fishing off this very pier. The wood's rotting a little now, but it's got some life left in it."

When they got closer, Mike adjusted his Yankees cap and looked out across the lake. "What's that in the water?"

"Where?" said Emily.

"Look in the water. Off the edge of the pier. There's something orange. A buoy maybe?"

Henry shielded his eyes from the sun with his hand. "Looks like a stray life jacket." Henry ventured closer. "Oh, no." He picked up the pace. "It's not just a life jacket. Come, help."

Mike said, "Someone's in the water!"

"Help me get him out." Henry got on his knees and pulled. Mike bent down and tugged along with him. A droopy head emerged. Henry yelled, "Help! Anyone hear me?" They struggled and eventually the shoulders appeared. "Call 911."

Susan grabbed her phone. "I don't know if he's breathing. Hurry. By the pier."

Henry shouted, "Tell them!" Henry struggled to breath as he pulled. "Tell them…Lake Pleasant…north side of the pier. By… the…boat rentals."

Susan relayed the message to the dispatcher, then tucked her phone in her cardigan pocket. She went closer, bent over, and stared at a limp body in wet flannel. Her legs wobbled. "Is he going to be okay?" She already knew the answer.

Henry and Mike grunted and partially stood up, pulling the

torso to the edge of the pier as though playing an intense game of tug of war. Emily ran over and grabbed the man's belt. "Susan, grab his waist. In front of Mike. Lean over and pull." Emily, out of breath, grunted as she spoke.

Henry said, "Stop." He took a slow breath. "When I say three, pull as hard as you can. One, two, three."

The plop of weight against the wood, the splashes of water, the smell of fish and seaweed…and finally the torso lay face down on the pier, covered in bits of pond scum. Henry and Mike grabbed the thighs and pushed him the rest of the way out of the water.

Susan screamed. "Oh, my God. Henry, do CPR! Turn him over." Her knees shook like Jell-O on a skateboard.

Mike unhooked the life vest and wriggled it over the man's head. His volunteer fire fighter training from back in the day kicked in. He and Henry rolled the man onto his back. He felt for a pulse. He stared at the chest hoping for a glimpse of movement, He listened, but already knew. "He's not breathing. We're too late."

A squad car arrived, then an ambulance. The officer asked them to stay back as he examined the scene. A second car screeched to a stop. A detective, a grown-up version of Opie from the old *Andy Griffith Show* and a family friend of Emily and Henry, hopped out. Susan thought she remembered him from the last time they visited. Maybe she was just thinking of the reruns.

The detective jogged over to the body, feeling for a pulse along the man's neck. He put his ear near the man's chest, then under his nose. With his head shaking, he checked the man's pockets, then stood up and looked into the water before approaching them.

Henry said, "Susan and Mike, this is Detective Ron Wooster."

Ron said, "We've met before. "You're the friends from New York, right?"

"That's us," said Mike. Susan nodded.

"What happened here? Did you see him fall in?" asked the detective.

"No. We went for a walk. Mike spotted the orange life vest and we all ran over," answered Henry. "It took all four of us to pull him out of the water. No signs of life."

"He's been in there a while. Did you hear or see anyone else near the pier?"

"No, said Henry.

Emily shook her head. "It was deserted, probably because of the weather earlier."

Susan had questions of her own. "Who is he?"

"There's no wallet or ID on him," said Ron.

"Was it a boating accident?" asked Susan.

Ron looked across the water. "I don't see a boat, do you?"

"Was he reported missing?" Susan felt her blood sugar drop and longed for a place to sit that didn't involve wriggling her body down to the ground. In her early sixties, she wasn't as limber as she once was and regretted not following through on the yoga classes she signed up for when she first retired.

Ron answered, "We haven't received any missing person reports."

The EMT, busy loading the body into the ambulance, called for the detective. "Wooster, come here. You have to see this."

When Ron was out of earshot, Susan said, "Why did he ask if we heard or saw anyone?"

Mike rolled his eyes. "Don't even start. Not again."

Susan said, "I'll bet this wasn't an accident. He suspects foul play."

Mike said, "He's just doing his job. No boat in sight, a man dead wearing a life jacket? Witnesses would help him figure out what happened, and I don't mean murder."

Emily said, "It is suspicious. What was he doing at the pier? I don't see a fishing pole and he wasn't wearing a bathing suit. Not that it's warm enough to swim." She hugged herself, trying to warm up now that the sun was on its way to setting. "Do you think he's done with us? This isn't a great start to a vacation for the two of you."

Susan said, "I don't mind." Not only didn't she mind, she felt her heart flutter. A death is sad; a murder is horrible. But there was nothing she loved more than a good mystery.

# Chapter 2

In spite of the eventful day, Susan slept well on the pull out couch in the living room. Yesterday had been exhausting—the long car ride...finding the body...staying up 'til midnight drinking wine with Emily and Henry...

She heard creaking as Emily climbed down the ladder from their loft bedroom.

Emily said, "How was the sofa bed? Where's Mike?"

"I slept like a log. Mike's in the kitchen, attempting to make coffee."

Henry scooted down the ladder. "I took the day off. How about we start with breakfast at The Outside Inn?"

Emily said, "Yes, Coralee was hoping to see you two again."

"I'm game," said Susan.

Mike came in. "I couldn't find coffee filters."

Susan said, "It's okay. We're going out for breakfast."

"Good. I make terrible coffee, anyway."

"Is Maddy coming with us?" asked Susan.

"No, she has school." Emily grabbed her jacket from the coat tree near the door. Henry grabbed his keys.

They piled into the Jeep. Susan wondered if the police had identified the dead man and, the cause of death. With the body bloated from the water, she couldn't tell if he had suffered an injury. *Maybe he had a heart attack and fell in. But if that were the case, why was he wearing a life jacket with no boat in sight? Life jacket?* If the circumstances hadn't been so morbid, she'd have laughed at the irony.

Henry pulled in front of The Outside Inn, a two-story yellow building with a wrap-around porch. On the way in, they passed a few guests sitting out front in Adirondack chairs, sipping coffee and reading the newspaper.

Silver-haired Coralee, the owner, greeted them in the lobby. She hugged Susan and Mike. "I hope you're hungry. The specials today are blueberry pancakes and pumpkin waffles. Of course, there are always eggs, toast, and cereal if you prefer."

Susan practically salivated at the thought of pumpkin waffles. They followed Coralee into the dining room and were seated in front of French doors which overlooked a golf course, currently littered with falling leaves.

Coralee said, "Did you hear what happened yesterday? About the man they found dead by the pier?"

"Hear about it?" said Emily. "Mike's the one who spotted him floating near the pier."

"You found him?"

"We sure did," said Henry. "I hoped I could revive him, but it was too late."

"Oh, my," said Coralee. "His poor wife is upstairs. She came to town to surprise him, and instead, *she* got the surprise—a visit from the local police!"

"Came to town?" said Emily. "They aren't local?"

"They live a few hours away, but her husband—her deceased husband—was up here on business."

"What kind of business?" asked Susan.

"I didn't ask."

"Ron said he didn't find a wallet. How did they identify him?" asked Susan. A dark-haired woman stopped at the table.

"Are you talking about my husband? My dead husband?" Her ebony eyes met Coralee's. "They found his car parked in the woods. That's how they identified him. Anything else you want to know?"

"I wasn't...I didn't mean to..." Coralee's face was as red as a ripe tomato.

"It's okay." The young widow wiped her eyes with the edge of her shirt. "This is big news. I'll bet murders don't happen every day in this sweet little town." She failed to conceal the sarcasm in her voice.

Coralee, visibly flustered, introduced them. "This is Kirby Taylor. Kirby, these are the people who found your husband's body yesterday."

"We're sorry for your loss," said Henry. He handed her his clean handkerchief.

"I'm so shaken. I don't know if I'm coming or going." The woman dabbed at her eyes.

"Would you like to join us for breakfast?" asked Henry.

She looked around the room, where no one sat solo. "Yeah. I suppose I should eat something. I have to go to the police station this morning and I'm dreading it. If I go upstairs, I'll just keep crying. I don't know how this happened. The police told me he was bludgeoned to death."

"Bludgeoned?" said Susan.

"They found injuries to his skull," said Kirby.

Henry pulled out a chair for Kirby. "We flipped him over so I could start CPR right away. Unfortunately, it was too late."

Coralee said, "What can I get you all for breakfast?" She wrote down their breakfast orders. "I'll have this out in a jiffy." She smoothed her apron on her way back to the kitchen.

"Do you know why he was wearing a life jacket? We didn't see a boat," said Susan.

"I have no idea," said Kirby. "He didn't know how to swim, so he generally avoided water."

"Could it have been related to his job?" said Emily.

"His job? He was an investment banker, not a marine biologist. He was here to meet with a client."

Susan said, "Do you have the name of his client?"

"Not with me. I suppose it's on his office computer. Back home."

Susan put her hand on Kirby's shoulder. "Do you have anyone you want us to call? Relatives? Friends?"

"I was hoping to go home today, but the detective said he couldn't release the body yet. I can call my sister. She'll drive up."

Coralee brought out breakfast. While the foursome devoured every bite of pumpkin waffles and blueberry pancakes, Kirby pushed scrambled eggs around on her plate.

Henry said, "Kirby, do you want us to go with you to the station?"

Kirby put down her fork. "Would you? I don't feel like I can drive right now."

"Of course."

Henry paid the bill, and led them to the parking lot where they all squeezed into his Jeep. Silence swaddled them like a weighted blanket.

Susan couldn't stand it. "I'm so sorry this happened. I'll bet you have tons of good memories together. How did you meet your husband?"

Kirby sniffled. "We met online. I'd tried that before and was about to give up when I saw Denver's profile. He seemed perfect. And he was." She sobbed. Susan felt bad for asking. Once again, words had shot out of her mouth without thinking. Kirby didn't stop crying until they pulled in front of the station.

Once inside, Ron said, "Have a seat in my office. I have more questions for everyone, but first, I need to take Ms. Taylor to officially identify the body." He looked at Kirby. "Are you up to it?"

Kirby nodded. "Let's get it over with." She followed the detective.

Susan said, "Just because they found the car, doesn't necessarily mean it's him."

Mike said, "Wishful thinking. I guess we'll know soon enough."

One of the officers offered them coffee while they waited. Susan could hardly drink it. And she thought Mike made terrible coffee?

When Ron returned with Kirby, she looked like a lost lamb. "It's Denver. He must be cold lying on that metal table. His face felt like rubber."

Emily said, "We're so sorry for your loss."

"I have to get out of here. Seeing him like that was harder than I could have imagined."

Henry said, "The detective wants to talk to us. Are you okay to wait, or should we come back later?" He looked at Ron. "We're her ride."

Ron said, "I'll have an officer bring her back to the inn." He motioned for the officer who had brought them coffee earlier.

"This way, ma'am."

After they were gone, Ron said, "I need to know every detail you can remember. It wasn't an accident. And, he didn't die of natural causes." Ron cleared his throat. "Denver Taylor was murdered."

"Murdered?" said Emily.

Susan said, "Someone killed him?" She already knew from Kirby that he'd been bludgeoned. So did Emily, for that matter.

"When the medical examiner got him cleaned up, he found skull injuries."

Emily said, "Injuries? Henry, you didn't notice a head wound, did you?"

"No, I guess I was too focused on whether or not I could revive him."

Ron said, "He was hit with a blunt object. Maybe an oar. Did you see one at the pier or on the shore?"

"No," said Emily. The others shook their heads.

"His car was parked half a mile away, hidden by evergreens," said Ron. "We ran the plates and got his ID from there."

The door flung open. A woman with a blond braid secured with a wooden hair clasp stormed in. An officer trailed behind her. "Stop! Ma'am, please…you can't go in there."

"It's okay. I've got this." Ron stood up. "Calm down, ma'am. Tell me what I can do for you."

"What you can do? *Now* you want to know what you can do? I want to see my husband."

"Your husband? Does he work at the station?" asked Ron. "Was he arrested?"

"Don't play dumb. I saw the story on the news this morning. Great way to find out. They showed his picture on TV; I know he's here. You could have told me my husband was murdered last night."

# Chapter 3

Susan felt the blood drain from her face. This couldn't be this woman's husband—it was Kirby Taylor's husband, Denver.

Ron said, "Calm down. There's been a mistake. We've already identified the victim."

"Who identified him? Shouldn't you have contacted the next of kin?"

"We did," said Ron. "She just left. Can I get your name?"

"Barb Rainer. And the victim, my husband, is—was, Chet Rainer."

Ron said, "It's not him. The victim's wife just identified him."

Barb shouted, "*I'm* his wife!" She took a breath and lowered her volume to little more than a whisper. "I wish I was wrong, but I'm not." She dabbed at her eyes with the sleeve of her camouflage jacket. "They showed his picture on TV."

Ron said, "Calm down. Can I get you a glass of water?"

"You think a glass of water is going to help? It's my husband. Chet Rainer." Barb Rainer whipped out her phone and held the screen in front of Ron's face. "See."

Ron squinted, then took the phone and squeezed the photo larger. "It certainly looks like him."

"And here," said the woman. "He left his wallet on the dresser. Check the driver's license. That's him."

The license read *Chet Rainer*. The address was local. Ron coughed a nervous cough. Susan handed him a glass of water which was sitting on his desk. "Would you be willing to identify the body," said Ron.

"Yes, of course."

Susan said, "When did he go missing?" Ron gave her a look as if to say he was the one asking questions here.

Barb sniffled. "He's a park ranger. Sometimes his days are long, and he doesn't always have cell service. When he didn't come home, I figured he was helping stranded campers or responding to a bear sighting. I went to bed. When I woke up, he hadn't come home. I turned on the news and…" She sobbed. Emily handed her a tissue from the box on Ron's desk. "I…I can't believe he's gone."

Ron said, "Before we go further, I'll have someone take you to him to verify the ID." Ron called the officer back in who'd taken Kirby to the morgue earlier.

"Take Mrs. Rainer downstairs to identify her husband's body."

"The one…"

"Yes," said Ron. "That one."

The officer shrugged his shoulders and escorted her out.

"Wow," said Susan. "How's that possible?"

Ron clicked the keys on his computer. "The license checks out. It's Chet Rainer."

"So, she's right. The victim is her husband," said Susan.

"I didn't say that." Ron squinted at the screen, then pushed back in his chair. "We've got a problem."

"I'll say," said Mike.

"Which problem?" asked Henry.

"The car's registered to Denver Taylor, and here's *his* license." The man in the photo wore glasses and his hair was brushed over to the side, but the resemblance was undeniable.

Henry said, "Are you sure it's the same person?"

"Denver Taylor has a small tattoo on his neck, see?" said Ron.

Henry said, "Pull up Chet Rainer's photo. I'm sure I saw a tattoo yesterday when I was trying to revive him."

Ron clicked the keys. "Here. Same tattoo as Denver. So small, it can barely be noticed." He motioned Henry closer to the screen. "Is this what you saw?"

"It is," said Henry.

Emily looked over Ron's shoulder. "Two identities?"

"Two wives?" said Susan.

"Two motives," said Ron.

Mike rubbed his head. "What about the wedding ring? The victim had a gold band on his finger. Whose ring is it, Denver's or Chet's?"

"I'll have to ask the wife. The wives." He picked up the desk phone to call the officer who'd escorted Barb. "Is the wife still with the body?"

The officer answered, "Yes, she's with him now."

"Go to the bag with the personal effects. Take out the wedding band and ask her if it's her husband's ring."

"Really?"

"Just do it. Call me as soon as you have an answer."

"What if it's not his ring?" said Emily.

"Hang on, I'm going to check marriage licenses." Ron searched and scrolled.

The officer called him back. "The wife says she's never seen the ring before."

"She's sure?"

"Yeah, and she's not too happy about it."

"Okay. You can see her out when she's done. I've got her contact information." Ron continued searching and scrolling.

Susan said, "Did you find anything?"

"Here's a marriage license for Chet Rainer. Looks like he married a Barbara Bacchus almost a decade ago." He clicked some more.

Emily said, "Okay, so Barb is the official wife. He's a bigamist."

"Not so fast," said Ron. "Chet Rainer died in 1998."

# Chapter 4

By the time they'd finished at the station, it was lunchtime. They headed back to the Jeep.

Susan said, "Those poor wives! You don't think they knew about each other, do you?"

Mike said, "Didn't look that way."

"This has all the hallmarks of a man leading a double life."

"Or, he's hiding something bigger," said Susan. "What if he's in witness protection?"

Mike said, "They don't give people in witness protection the identity of a dead person. And, I think they only get to bring one wife."

"Anyhow," said Henry, "the two of you came for a visit, so let's not waste the whole day on the murder." He opened the Jeep with a chirp of the key and they slid in.

"There's a new café downtown next to the bookstore," said Emily. "Let's grab a bite to eat and browse the shops."

Henry cleared his throat. "You know how much I love aimless shopping." He started up the Jeep.

Emily said, "We'll compromise. After lunch, Susan and I will take a quick browse while you two grab a latte at the bookstore."

Henry shrugged. "Whatever."

Susan said, "Barb and Chet were married, legally or not, for ten years. Can you imagine how angry Barb would be if she found out her husband had a second—not to mention younger—wife?"

Emily said, "I peeked at the computer screen over Ron's shoulder. Barb Rainer lives in an area that's all farmland at the edge of town."

"Was her husband a park ranger? Kirby said he was an investment banker. She came up to surprise him. What if she saw him with Barb and put two and two together?" asked Susan.

"If so, she hid it well," said Henry. "Ron said the car was found in the woods, half a mile or so from the pier where we found him. Why didn't he park closer to the water? He was wearing a life jacket. He must have intended to get on a boat, or go for a swim."

"Kirby said he didn't know how to swim," said Emily. "If you couldn't swim, would you go boating by yourself?"

The downtown area was as quaint as a china tea cup in an antique shop. Maple Street ran through the main drag which sported—amongst other shops—a bookstore, overpriced clothing boutiques, a jewelry store, a fudge shop… The canopied café was white, matching the other storefronts.

"We're here," said Henry.

They passed a chalkboard easel listing the specials on their way in. The aroma of freshly baked bread and cookies wafted through the door.

"I'm definitely having some of that bread," said Emily. "I noticed a veggie sandwich on the menu outside."

Susan said, "A turkey and sliced squash sandwich. Hmm."

They were seated at a booth, and no one had trouble finding

something delicious for lunch. After the food arrived, they continued speculating over the murder case. Emily wrote true crime books, and Henry loved puzzles. Susan knew they wouldn't mind dwelling on the murder, at least for a little while.

Henry said, "Suppose Barb got suspicious for whatever reason and followed Chet into the woods. She confronts him, they argue, she gets angry, she hits him over the head."

"And drags him half a mile to the pier, puts a life jacket on him, and tosses him into the water?" asked Emily. "Henry, I'm disappointed in you."

"I'm a little rusty, what can I say?"

Emily said, "If she followed him into the woods, she must have followed him all the way to the pier, then killed him."

Susan said, "I wonder if he was alone in the car and why he was there in the first place."

Emily said, "I'll bet the car hasn't been moved yet."

"What are you thinking, Emily? We can't go near the crime scene," said Henry.

"But, we can trace the path from where they found the car, to the pier. Maybe they missed something. It's a gorgeous day for a hike. After Susan and I shop, of course."

After lunch, Henry and Mike headed next door to get coffee at the bookstore while the ladies shopped. Neither Henry nor Mike wanted coffee, but it beat trekking around the stores.

The shop next to the bookstore had colorful giraffes painted on the window. Emily said, "I bought a shower gift for a co-worker here. You might find something here for Mia and Annalise—or for the half-pint on the way."

Susan loved nothing more than spoiling her granddaughters. A bell over the door tinkled. An atomizer perched near the register spewed lavender mist throughout the shop.

"Let me know if I can help with anything," said the woman behind the counter. "What sizes are you looking for?"

Susan said, "My granddaughters are four and seven. And, there's a newborn on the way. My daughter either doesn't know, or isn't sharing the baby's sex. She says they want to be surprised, but Lynette generally hates surprises."

"I made the onesies over here out of baby crib quilts. I call them Quiltamas—you know, like pajamas and quilts put together."

Emily said, "What a cute portmanteau."

"A what?" said the owner.

"Sorry, it's the writer/college professor in me. *Portmanteau* is when you combine two words into one, like brunch, or motel."

"You should go on *Shark Tank*," said Susan. "I love that show."

The woman straightened the pile. "Nowadays, they tell parents not to put blankets in the cribs, but it gets chilly in the winter." She stopped and looked up at Susan. "You think *Shark Tank* would invite me?"

"It's worth a try." Susan ran her hand over the colorful onesie. "It's so soft! I'll take this one with the pink and yellow bunnies." She flipped through the stack and pulled out another. "And this one with the butterflies."

"Perfect. I'm glad there are people in the world who haven't hopped on the gender neutral bandwagon. Not that there's anything wrong with gender neutral, but I still love the idea of pink for girls and blue for boys. Call me old fashioned."

"Do you have more newborn items," asked Susan.

"Right around the corner."

Susan and Emily started around the corner, but stopped in their tracks. A woman in dark wash jeans and a suede jacket hummed as she flipped through the clothing. Susan whispered, "Isn't that Kirby Taylor? She's looking at layette items. I'd have thought

24

she'd be too upset to go shopping. She was a wreck after identifying her husband's body this morning."

Emily whispered back, "I'm wondering why she's looking at baby clothes. Do you think…"

"Do I think she's pregnant? She didn't look like it this morning. I can't tell with the jacket."

Susan said, "Why else would she be in here?"

"To buy something for a niece or nephew, or godchild or…"

"Okay, okay. Come on."

Susan went right up to Kirby. "I'm glad you're feeling better than when we left you."

Kirby jumped. "You startled me. I had to get out of the inn. I was sitting alone, crying. Thought a distraction would help."

Susan said, "Are you shopping for someone special, or are you expecting your own little bundle of joy?"

She patted her stomach over her jacket. "I just found out a few days ago. I drove up here to surprise Denver. I never got to tell him." She pulled a tissue out of her jacket pocket.

Susan said, "That's so sad."

"Well, at least a part of him will live on," said Kirby.

Susan said, "Check out the Quiltamas up front."

"I'll do that." Kirby went up front, paid, and left. Susan picked up two pink hoodies with embroidered flowers, then, exchanged the pink one for a light blue one with a sailboat appliqué.

"Ready to go?" asked Emily.

"I am." Susan handed the owner at the register a credit card. "I'll take the Quiltamas and these hoodies."

Emily said, "Poor Kirby. Imagine knowing the love of your life died without knowing he had a child on the way."

The owner looked up from ringing the hoodie in her hand. "What are you talking about? The woman who was just in here?

The one who looks like Selena Gomez?"

"Yes," said Emily. "She just lost her husband. You must have seen it on the news."

"Oh, my God! That was her husband who was murdered? They were just in here together a few days ago. And she came in today chatting about how she was going to decorate the nursery."

Susan's ears twitched. "A few days ago? With her husband? Two of them together?"

"Yeah. I didn't realize he was the one who'd been murdered."

"They came in shopping for baby clothes together?" asked Susan. "He knew she was pregnant?"

"Yes. I thought to myself, that marriage isn't going to last. The poor baby will wind up in a broken home."

"They didn't get along?" said Susan.

"They had a big fight right back there where you picked up the hoodies."

"What were they fighting about?" asked Emily.

"I was trying to mind my own business, but it was kind of hard given the volume and the size of this place. She said he'd never see his child and he'd be sorry. He said she was all hot air and angry because she'd been so naïve."

Susan said, "You should tell the police. She told them she'd come to Sugarbury Falls to surprise him but he was dead before she could. And she never mentioned being pregnant."

Emily handed the owner a business card. "This number will get you through to the detective handling the case. His name is Ron Wooster."

# Chapter 5

Henry picked up Susan and Emily in front of the baby store. "Did you have fun?"

Emily said, "We did. Susan found some cute items for Annalise and Mia. But, listen to what we found out."

Mike said, "Let me guess. You found out no store can keep enough inventory on hand when Susan's shopping for our grandkids."

Susan gave him a swat. "Very funny. We ran into Kirby Taylor."

Emily said, "She's pregnant! And, she already met with Denver. She told us she came to surprise him, but the owner at the baby store said she and Denver had a big argument right in the store, the day before he was murdered."

Henry said, "If Kirby lied about when and why she came to town, there's no telling what else she lied about."

Mike said, "Why didn't she say she was pregnant back at the station? And she didn't say anything about a fight."

Henry parked the Jeep at the pier. "Not sure what we're

looking for, but let's give it a whirl."

They got out of the Jeep and followed the worn gravel path into the woods. Leaves crunched under their feet; tree limbs snapped liked dry bones.

Henry said, "If you find something, don't pick it up. We don't want to contaminate potential evidence." He led the way, scrutinizing each step until the path forked. "Which way?"

Emily said, "I've been running on these paths. Only the one on the left widens enough to accommodate a car." She stepped over a fallen branch.

Mike said, "I see crime scene tape up ahead."

Susan said, "That's the car! Come on."

Henry said, "Remember, we can't cross the tape."

"But, we can peek into the car windows from back here," said Susan. She found she couldn't. Her knees creaked as she passed underneath the tape. A crocheted knitted hat with a multi-colored tassel stared up at her from the floor of the passenger seat.

"Hey. He must have had a female passenger," said Susan.

Mike said, "You know you weren't supposed to go…"

"Yeah, but good thing I did."

"How do you figure?" said Mike. "The car's going to the police lab. They'll see it soon enough. If it's even Kirby's hat; she could have left it in the car weeks ago," said Mike.

Emily said, "Let's walk back to the pier. Maybe we missed something."

Henry said, "Yeah. And let's stop at the boat rental place. I have a hunch."

They trudged through the path and took a detour leading to the boat rental shack. Two men got out of a boat, holding fishing rods and a cooler. They carried orange life vests with them into the rental shack.

"What are we waiting for?" said Susan. She was the first to the door. They waited while the owner checked the fishermen back in, then she approached the register.

"Excuse me."

"Can I help you?"

"I hope so."

"What kind of boat are you looking for?" asked the man. "Will you need fishing gear? There's a discount if you rent both together."

Susan said, "Which boat did you rent to a gentleman named Denver Taylor a day or two ago?" She hesitated. "Or, he may have gone by Chet Rainer."

The owner put the returned fishing poles back on the wall. "I already went through this with the police. Who are you?"

"Susan. Susan Wiles. We found the body. And we promised his wife we'd find out what we could. She's pregnant, you know."

"I'll tell you what I told the police. I never saw the dead guy. They showed me a photo. I have no record of him renting a boat, ever."

"But he was found wearing a life jacket. It looks like one of yours." Susan pointed to the just returned vest lying on the counter. "When you rent a boat to someone, looks like you give them the life vests in here."

"If you leave them in the boat, they grow legs. Learned that lesson early on. As far as the dead guy wearing one, all life jackets look alike."

"No, it had your logo on it," said Susan. Mike put his hand on her shoulder as if to slow her down.

Emily said, "Did you rent any boats that were not returned to you?"

The owner said, "Just one. It's still missing."

"Who rented it?" asked Emily. "It's important."

"Some woman."

"Can you describe her?" asked Emily.

"She was wearing a parka and her hair was stuffed inside a knit hat."

"Was she tall or short?" asked Susan. "Young, or old?"

"I don't know. Average, I guess."

Mike said, "Can you check your receipts and get a name?"

"She paid cash. I remember because it was a multi-day rental and it cost a pretty penny. Had to leave a deposit, too. She never came back for it, like that's a surprise. It won't cover the cost of me replacing the boat."

Henry handed the man a business card. "If you think of anything, please call me, or better yet, call the police."

Susan said, "And if we find your boat, we'll let you know."

They left the shop and walked back toward the pier. Mike said, "If we find his boat? Seriously, Susan?"

She shrugged her shoulders. "You never know."

Back at the pier, Emily said, "Let's take one last look around here. We have to be missing something." She crouched down and examined the wood. Mike examined the area around the pier, and Susan looked into the water.

Henry went under the pier and checked the underside. "Hey, come here! I found something. It's stuck on the wood." He took a leather glove out of his pocket and freed it. "Don't touch."

They all rushed over. Mike said, "It looks like a hair clasp."

"Exactly," said Susan. "The same kind of hair clasp Barb Rainer had in her hair when we saw her at the station!"

# Chapter 6

On the way home, they stopped at the police station. Ron brought them into his office.

Henry said, "I found this stuck under the pier where we found the body."

Susan chimed in. "It belongs to Barb Rainer."

"How do you know it's hers?" asked Ron.

Susan said, "It's handmade. Barb wore it the day she stormed in here demanding to see her husband."

Ron pulled an evidence bag out of his drawer. "Anyone could have dropped this at any time."

Henry said, "It was stuck on the slats underneath the pier. The slats aren't large enough for it to have fallen through from the surface."

Ron sighed. "Even if it belongs to Barb Rainer, we'll have a hard time getting prints or DNA off it to prove it. Who knows how long it's been there? It doesn't mean she killed him even if she was there."

"We were hoping it was a lead," said Susan.

"And I appreciate it, but know we've gone over the area thoroughly."

"Not thoroughly enough to find the hair clip," said Susan.

Mike put his hand on Susan's shoulder and nudged her toward the door. "Come on."

Ron said, "There's a killer out there somewhere. The last thing I'd want is for any of you to get hurt."

Emily said, "Thanks for your time."

On the way home, Susan said, "I know we're on to something."

"You heard the detective," said Mike.

Susan said, "The hair clasp at the pier places Barb at the scene. I'm sure of it. He should at least bring her in for questioning."

"You heard what he said," said Henry. "If it's hers, which he probably can't prove, it means she was there at some point in time. Not necessarily the night of the murder."

"Let it go," said Mike.

Back at the house, Emily took Susan aside. "My neighbor, Rebecca, is a tech whiz. I swear she's either CIA or a corporate spy. I'll give her a call." Emily took her phone into the kitchen while the others chatted in the living room.

Mike said, "If Chet Rainer died in the nineties, is the marriage legal?"

Henry shrugged his shoulders. The doorbell rang. "Em, are we expecting anyone?"

Emily said, "I'll get it." Thirty-something Rebecca, dressed in jeans and a Yale sweatshirt, stood in the door with a laptop tucked under her arm.

Henry whispered to Emily. "I thought we were going to drop this?"

Emily said, "Susan and Mike, this is our neighbor, Rebecca. Rebecca and her wife just adopted a baby girl. I'm glad she could take time out to come over, being a busy mom and working full time."

"Abby's watching Carly," said Rebecca. "I'm happy to help."

"Help with what?" asked Henry.

Emily jumped in. "Just some technical stuff." She turned to Rebecca. "Have a seat." Rebecca sat on the sofa and opened her laptop. "Where should we start?"

Emily sat beside her. "Can you check out a Barb Rainer?"

Henry said, "Might be under Barbara, not Barb."

"Is she local?" asked Rebecca.

"Yes," said Emily.

"And do the same with Kirby Taylor," added Susan.

Rebecca clicked and scrolled. In the blink of an eye, she found information. "Barbara Rainer. She was born here, stayed local for college. Married to a Chet Rainer." She clicked to another screen. "They bought a house together."

"Anything else?" asked Emily.

Rebecca searched. "She has a gun permit. So does he."

"Interesting. And what about Kirby Taylor?" asked Emily.

"Kirby Taylor. Local?" asked Rebecca.

"From Vermont," said Emily, "but not local."

"Age?" asked Rebecca.

Susan said, "I'd guess mid to late thirties."

"Here's a Natalie Kirby Taylor. Think that's her?" asked Rebecca. She showed them a driver's license photo on the screen.

"That's her!" said Susan.

"She has a criminal record."

"For what?" asked Henry.

"She assaulted one of her sorority sisters in college. It happened fifteen years ago. Nothing since then."

Henry said, "What can you find on a Denver Taylor?"

Rebecca searched. "Denver. D-e-n-v-e-r?"

Henry nodded. "There should be a marriage and driver's license. And can you find out his occupation? The wife says he was an investment banker."

"Well," said Rebecca, "Denver Taylor is too young to drive, and definitely too young to be married. He had his second birthday last month."

"Seriously?" said Susan. "So whoever the victim is, he assumed a dead man's identity to become Chet Rainer, and stole a baby's identity to become Denver Taylor. How did he manage to keep it hidden to not one, but two wives?"

Rebecca said, "Maybe they saw what they wanted to see."

"Can you print off a picture of both wives?" asked Emily. "The guy at the boat rental might recognize one of them."

Susan said, "We think Barb Rainer killed him. We found her hair clasp near where we found the body."

"What's the time frame for the murder?" asked Rebecca.

Henry said, "My best friend is the medical examiner. He says the victim was killed the night before we found him."

"He was wearing a life jacket which came from the boat rental shack," added Susan. "But they haven't found a boat."

"Don't all life jackets look alike?" asked Rebecca.

"It had the business logo printed on it," said Susan.

Mike said, "Someone rented a boat the previous day, but it was never returned. We're guessing he'd been in that boat."

"Otherwise, why would he have been wearing the life vest from the rental shack," said Susan.

"The boat was rented and missing before the murder occurred," said Rebecca. "When did you find the body?"

"The following afternoon," said Henry.

"No one found the body earlier than mid-afternoon?" asked Rebecca.

"It stormed earlier in the day. The sun came out just before Susan and Mike arrived," said Henry.

"The boat was rented by a woman," said Emily. "The owner of the boat rental shack says she was bundled up and he couldn't describe her, but I'm hoping if we show him photos, it might jog his memory."

Susan said, "The other possibility is that Kirby Taylor murdered him. What kind of car does she drive?"

"A blue, late-model Camry," said Rebecca.

"How about *her* husband, Denver Taylor? They found his car not far from the murder scene."

She clicked more keys. "He drives a white Nissan."

Emily nodded. "That's the car they found in the woods."

"And Barb Rainer?" Susan knew she was asking a lot of questions, but Rebecca didn't seem to mind. *Maybe she welcomes the break from caring for an infant. When Lynette and Evan were babies, I cherished pockets of alone time, though I loved them to death.*

"A black, Ford pick-up truck."

"I wish we knew where Kirby and Barb were the night of the murder," said Emily.

"Where did Kirby stay? You said she isn't local"

"At the Outside Inn," said Emily.

"Does Coralee have CCTV?" asked Rebecca.

"Yes, she does," said Emily. "But I don't know how long she keeps the footage."

Rebecca said, "Shops and hotels generally keep the footage at least 30 days."

Mike said, "That won't help us nail down Barb Rainer's

whereabouts. I'm sure Ron questioned both of them."

"And the grieving widows could have said they were alone and no one saw them all night," said Mike.

Susan said, "Then, both wives will thank us for double checking their alibis and finding the real killer."

# Chapter 7

The next morning, Henry took Mike to play golf. Susan and Emily ate breakfast and ran over to the inn after Coralee's breakfast rush. Susan smelled the aroma of coffee and bacon lingering in the air the moment they entered the lobby.

Coralee said, "Good morning. Did you all eat?"

"We grabbed a bite at home," said Emily.

"Well, there's coffee and pastries if you're still hungry. You said you needed information. I found the security tape. What else do you need?"

"Which day did Kirby Taylor check in?" asked Emily.

Coralee wiped her hands on her apron "Kirby Taylor checked in on the 27th."

Emily said, "That's three days before we found the body. We know she was at the baby shop with Denver on the 28th, but she claimed she never got the chance to see him. Why did she lie?"

Coralee shrugged her shoulders.

Susan said, "According to the baby shop owner, Kirby and

Denver argued in the baby store. Maybe she told him to take a hike."

Emily said, "Coralee, was Denver here with Kirby on the 28th?"

"Sorry, Emily. It's not like I hang out on the porch watching my guests' comings and goings."

"Which brings us to why we're here," said Emily. "Can we see the CCTV footage for the 29th?"

"Come on back." Coralee led them behind the front desk into her office. "I've got it cued up for you." She started the video. "Kirby's car is the blue Camry. You can see it there in the parking lot."

"Fast forward," said Emily. "Stop. There. Kirby's going out. Go slow. She isn't using her car. Looks like she's heading to the golf course."

Coralee said, "There's a walking trail back there. One of those with the fitness stations. A lot of guests take walks out there, especially with the changing leaves at this time of year."

Emily said, "We lost her."

"The cameras don't reach past that point." Coralee fast forwarded. "Hold on." She pressed the fast forward button. "There she is. She returns an hour later, look at the time stamp."

Emily sighed. "She couldn't have walked back and forth to the boat rental in that amount of time. Keep going."

Coralee said, "Her car stays parked in the lot all night."

"Did she come down for breakfast the morning of the 30th?" asked Susan. "That's the day we found the body."

"She generally ordered room service. Let me look at her bill." Coralee switched to another screen. "She ordered breakfast the morning of the 30th at 8 a.m. so she was here in the morning."

The bell on the front desk rang insistently. Coralee ducked out of the office to see what was going on. "Kirby? Is something wrong?"

"I want to leave. Right now. I want to settle my bill and hit the road." Her anger turned to tears.

Emily said, "I know you're upset about your husband—of course you would be—but you don't look like you should drive right now."

"If you knew…If I…oooh." Kirby punched her fist on the counter and tears streamed down her cheeks.

Coralee went around to the front of the desk and put her arm around her. "Let's go out on the porch. The fresh air will do you good."

They pulled up Adirondack chairs around a low wooden table. Emily and Susan sat on the porch swing. Susan said, "What happened this morning?"

"The detective asks me to come to the station. He shows me a wedding ring and I tell him I've never seen it before. Then, he asks all sorts of questions about Denver. When and where did we meet, did I ever see him at the investment banking office or meet any of his work colleagues? How often did he go out of town? Stuff like that."

"And did you answer his questions?" asked Susan.

"I told him Denver commuted to the city by train every day. I never made the long ride to see him at work. Why would I have? I don't know any of his colleagues."

"Are they releasing his body to you?" asked Susan.

"That's just it. They have to release it to the next of kin, which, wouldn't you assume is me? But, no. The detective says—get this —he has another wife! One who lives here in town. They've been married ten years! Ten years! I feel like I'm in some sort of cruel nightmare."

"You poor thing," said Susan.

"I was such a fool. I had a gut feeling. Truthfully, I followed him up here to check up on him."

"Check up on him? What made you suspicious?"

"Last week he told me he went to Chicago for business. I found gas and restaurant receipts for purchases made in Vermont during the dates he was supposed to have been in Chicago. Then, when he was out, I checked his phone. He had a bunch of calls back and forth to 'boss.' I called the number, and a woman answered. It wasn't a place of business. I heard *The View* on the TV in the background."

"Did you say anything to the woman?" asked Emily.

"No, I hung up."

Susan said, "Maybe the boss was home sick that day."

Kirby said, "I asked Denver if his boss was a man or a woman. Of course, I didn't tell him why I was asking. He said his boss was a man."

"Did you believe him?" asked Susan.

"Of course not. I looked up the bank's website. The head manager is a man, like he said. So, I decided to follow him this trip. I checked his GPS while he was in the shower, and here I am. I'm such a fool." She started sobbing again. "You know the first place he stopped when he got here? A farm house. I figured it was his mistress, but now I know it was his wife."

"Did you confront him?" asked Susan.

"No, I checked in here. I called him. I told him I was in town and had a surprise for him and to meet me at the baby shop. Boy, did he sound rattled. I loved it."

Emily said, "What happened when you saw him?"

"I told him I was pregnant right there in the shop. You should have seen his face."

Susan said, "Was he happy? Mad? Stunned?"

"Stunned, then he got angry. We had a fight right there in public. I told him I never wanted to see him again."

"How long have you been married?" asked Emily.

"I don't suppose I am married! The detective said Denver Taylor isn't even his real name. I don't know the name of my baby's father!"

Coralee hugged her like a mother comforting a hurt child. "It's going to all be okay."

Kirby sobbed, "Now I have a baby coming and I'll be raising it all on my own."

"You've got plenty of time to sort it all out," said Coralee. "Why don't I bring you a cup of tea and you relax a while before taking off on a long trip."

"I…I'll be in my room."

"Wait," said Susan. "Did you see him the day he was murdered?"

"I didn't see him after that. Not until I saw his body at the police station."

Coralee said, "Well, go get some rest now. I'll bring a cup of tea to your room.

Susan said, "CCTV shows her car was in the lot all evening. Isn't that an alibi?"

Coralee said, "And she ordered breakfast the next morning. I have the receipt."

Emily said, "And she seemed truly surprised to find out her husband is a bigamist. I don't think she killed him."

# Chapter 8

The next morning, Henry said, "I have to go into work for a couple of hours, but I should be home by lunchtime. Let's have a picnic by the lake. It's supposed to be a beautiful day."

"Sure," said Emily. "Sounds good."

When Henry arrived at the emergency room, two patients were waiting to see a doctor. While treating a young boy's asthma attack, a nurse came into the cubicle and pulled him aside.

"There's a woman in triage. She thinks she's having a heart attack. Her pulse is elevated, she has chest pain, and she feels nauseated."

"Stay with this boy. He needs to finish the breathing treatment," said Henry. He went to the woman, who he recognized from the police station. He checked the intake form. It was Barb Rainer, the victim's original wife. He told the nurse to get set up for an EKG and ordered bloodwork.

"Good morning, what's going on? The nurse says you're having chest pain."

"I…I feel like I'm going to die. My chest hurts, I can't breathe."

He listened to her heart. "When did this start?"

"About an hour ago. I woke up with chest pain and it got worse when I got out of bed, then I couldn't catch my breath. I'm lucky I made it here. I thought about calling an ambulance."

The nurse hooked her up to the EKG machine.

Henry said, "Have you had this pain before? Are you on any medications?"

"No. I barely take aspirin when I get a headache."

"Have you been under any unusual stress lately?"

"My husband was murdered. Does that count?"

"Chet Rainer, right? I saw you at the police station."

She sat up. "You're the one who found him. I recognize you."

"Yes. I'm sorry for your loss. The EKG looks normal." He listened to her heart and lungs. "My guess is you had a panic attack. Are you feeling better?"

"A little better. A panic attack? That's all this is?"

"It can feel like you're dying; it's no joke. I can write you a prescription for something to relax you."

"I don't like taking pills."

"Just in case you need it during this crisis period. Death of a spouse is a traumatic event in itself, but when it was violent and unexpected, even more so."

"I was handling his death. It's the other shock that got to me."

"What other shock?" Henry knew, but of course, didn't let on.

"My husband had a second wife who lives a few hours from here. Not an ex-wife or former wife, but another current wife. Can you imagine? I was such a fool, not seeing it. And that's not all. Chet Rainer wasn't even his real name. I was married for ten years to someone I didn't know at all."

"Don't beat yourself up. I'm sure he went to great lengths to hide it."

"Even lied about his career. Park ranger, my foot. All those long days with no cell service, he was off with his second wife."

"I'm so sorry you're going through this."

"And, he took out a second mortgage on our home without telling me. Not only is he dead, he left me in debt. I'm hoping I can sell the family fishing cabin out on Fisherman's Cove. It's falling apart, but it's right on the lake. It might be of use to someone. Other than that, I don't know what to do about his debts. It's not like I've got fancy jewelry or other property to sell. Do you know anyone who wants to buy a Ford pick-up truck?"

"I'll keep my ears open."

"I don't bring in enough to live on selling handmade jewelry and hair ornaments on Etsy. The jerk didn't have life insurance. And I counted on him having a state pension, you know, from the park ranger job."

"I can give you a referral to a therapist."

"So, you think I'm crazy?"

"Of course not. You're going through a difficult time. It might help to talk to someone, or to learn coping strategies, that's all."

"Thanks, but no thanks. As long as I know I'm not dying, I'll be okay."

"Come back if it happens again."

After finishing with Barb Rainer, Henry had a few minutes to himself. He called Emily.

"Em, I just saw Barb Rainer at the hospital. Something she said is nagging at me. Is Rebecca is available this morning?"

Emily called Rebecca as soon as she finished talking with Henry. Rebecca came over with Carly in a carriage.

"Thanks, Rebecca. I hate to keep bothering you, but Henry thinks this is important."

"I like playing private eye. Besides, I have a little time before my Biztech conference call. What do you need?"

"Henry says Barb Rainer mentioned a family fishing cabin on the lake. Maybe that's where she's keeping the boat. Can you find out exactly where the cabin is?"

"I'll give it a whirl." She opened her laptop. "Barbara Rainer, right?"

"Yes. It was a family property."

Rebecca clicked and scrolled. "Where are your friends?"

"They went over to the country store and corn maze. Maddy's playing tour guide. Thought they'd have a little fun while we waited for Henry to get home. I was going to do some writing, but couldn't get my head into it."

Rebecca clicked and scrolled. "The only property I see with her name on it is a house she co-owns with Chet Rainer. Did you know there's a second mortgage on the property?"

"Henry mentioned it. Maybe you should try Barb's maiden name. You had it on the marriage license, do you remember?"

"Yeah. Bacchus. Barbara Bacchus." She clicked and scrolled. "There's a property under the name Charles Bacchus."

"Maybe that's her father."

"Yeah." Rebecca continued. "He's deceased. Looks like Barb was their only child."

"And Barb's mother?"

"Also deceased." She continued. "Here you go. The property passed on to Barbara Bacchus in 2011."

Emily moved in closer. "That's on Lake Pleasant."

"Yes, it is," said Rebecca. "I'll pull up Google Maps, give me a minute. Here we go. Have a look."

"Like I thought. Fisherman's Cove. It's across the lake from the pier. Can you print it?"

"Sure."

Emily picked up her phone. "Ron, it's Emily Fox. I got a tip you might want to check out regarding the missing boat."

"We've searched the whole area and haven't come up with anything," said Ron.

"Barb Rainer owns a fishing cabin near the water. It was passed down to her just like Henry got this place from his parents and it's a bit remote judging by the map. I can text you the location."

"We already checked it out. No boat."

"Fisherman's Cove. It's around the bend; maybe your guys missed it?"

"No, Emily. We got the right location. It's abandoned. No one's been there in years. All we found were three inches of dust and windows nearly opaque from dirt."

Emily said, "Did Barb have an alibi for the night her husband was murdered?"

Ron said, "I can't discuss an ongoing case, Emily. I've already said too much."

"But, we found the body. And you know from past experience we'll keep anything you say confidential. Let us help."

"If it'll get you off my back, I'll say this. Barb Rainer has an alibi. She was downtown at a bible study class the evening he was murdered. Now, thanks for the tip, but try to enjoy your time with your friends and leave the detective work to me, okay?"

"Okay."

Rebecca said, "Sounds like he wasn't interested."

"Sorry for wasting your time. I have a gut feeling about this, but if she has an alibi, and the boat isn't parked on her lakeside property, I guess I'm wrong."

"What's the alibi?" asked Rebecca.

"She was at bible study."

"Which church?"

"I don't know. He said she was downtown at bible study."

"Abby goes to bible study. Her church is downtown. Maybe they know each other. I'll ask." She tucked the blanket around Carly, who'd been asleep in the carriage the whole time, and headed back home.

Emily loaded the dishes and mopped the kitchen floor. She thought out loud, with Chester watching her from his perch on the counter.

*Both wives had alibis. Neither knew about the bigamy until after he died. Barb told Henry she was unaware that Chet took out a second mortgage on their home. We found the hair clip, but if she sells them on Etsy, there's no telling who else may have purchased one. Not without accessing Barb's sale records.*

She called Rebecca. "One more thing. Can you hack into Etsy sales records to see if anyone bought that hair clip I told you about that we found at the pier?"

"Piece of cake. And, I asked Abby about her church. She knows Barb Rainer. Thinks she's a nice lady who could never commit murder. Anyhow, I'll text you the name and address of the church."

"Thanks, Rebecca. Is that Carly crying?"

"Yeah, and since Abby watched her all morning, I'd better go."

As tempted as she was to run over to the church and verify Barb's alibi, she knew she shouldn't. Besides, other than the pastor, it's unlikely anyone else would be there in the middle of the day. No, if she were going to check, she'd have to show up during bible study. She wondered how Abby would feel about having her tag along.

"Hey, I'm home," said Henry. He scruffed Spunky's fur, then kissed Emily. "Where's everybody?"

"Still at the corn maze. Hope they didn't get lost."

No sooner had she said it, Maddy, Susan, and Mike came through the door.

"Did you have fun?" asked Emily.

Susan said, "It was a blast. Maddy and I got a little turned around, but Mike had his head on straight. Once we listened to him, we found our way out."

Maddy said, "I could have used the GPS on my phone, but I didn't. We did it the old fashioned way, following the sun and praying to the Gods. Like you did when you were a kid, right Dad?"

"Very funny. I mean LOL. See, I'm up on the times. I know the lingo."

Susan said, "We'll have to come back with Annalise and Mia. They'd have a blast."

Henry said, "You'll have to hurry if you want to get it in this year. He closes it up over the winter. Speaking of winter, it's not too chilly out. Are we still doing that picnic?"

# Chapter 9

By the time they got themselves together and packed a picnic basket, it was close to supper time. "I have a great idea," said Emily. "Why don't we rent a boat and take our picnic across the lake."

"Across the lake, say, to where Barb Rainer owns a cabin?" asked Henry.

"Oh, Barb owns a cabin there?"

Henry shook his head. "Em, you know I'm onto you."

"But it sounds like a lovely idea," said Susan. "I'll grab the picnic basket. Mike, grab the cooler."

Spunky barked. Henry said, "I think he wants to come along." He snapped on the leash and grabbed Spunky's water bowl. "Are you coming, Maddy?"

"No, I'm going to stay here. I have a research paper due on Monday. Can I order a pizza?"

Henry pulled his debit card out of his wallet. "Sure. And if you want to invite Brooke or Jessica over, go for it."

They arrived at the boat rental office and rented a small

motorized row boat. Spunky jumped in and made himself comfortable. It was a tight squeeze for four adults in bulky life vests, but they managed. The child-sized life jacket fit Spunky to a tee.

Susan said, "You're lucky living so close to the water. Mike, maybe we should sell our place and move here when you retire."

"Like you'd move away from Lynette and the grandkids? You couldn't do it."

Emily said, "But you're always welcome to visit us. You could stay a few weeks if you'd like. And bring the girls. They'd have a blast."

"I'll keep it in mind," said Susan. She daydreamed about picking strawberries and taking the girls swimming at the pier. They passed a playground on the way to the lake.

Henry slowed the boat down. "How about right here? There's a nice stretch of grass."

Emily said, "How about up there?" She pulled out the directions Rebecca printed for her. "Around the curve, jag left."

"You mean Fisherman's Cove?"

"Is that what they call it?" asked Emily.

Henry shook his head, then complied. He tied the boat to a rickety pier over shallow water and helped the others out. Spunky hopped out as if he still had all four of his legs. His tail wagged as he sniffed the new surroundings and followed Emily and Susan to the grass where they spread out the picnic blanket. Susan, feeling as worn out as the pier where they docked, and envious of the dog's agility, tried her best to get down to the ground gracefully.

Mike pulled out the bottle of wine he'd stuck in the cooler. Susan grabbed the Styrofoam cups from the picnic basket. "A toast to good friends," said Mike.

They munched on egg salad sandwiches, cold pasta salad, chips, and Maddy's homemade pumpkin bread. Henry had slipped Spunky's rubber ball into his pocket on the way out and tossed it to the dog's delight. The sun sparkled on the water as it sank lower in the sky.

Henry said, "Won't be many days warm enough for a picnic before winter settles in."

Susan's legs ached to move. "Want to take a walk and see what's around?"

Emily jumped up. "Sure." She tucked the leftover food and utensils back into the basket and cooler. Henry and Mike gathered the garbage and folded the blanket. Then, they followed the path to the cabin.

The cabin looked as though it hadn't been painted in years. The wood around the doorframe crumbled from rot. "This is more of a shack rather than a cabin, isn't it?" said Emily. She walked around the side and looked in the window. "There's so much dirt caked on the windows, I can't see what's inside."

Susan turned the front door handle. "It's locked, but I don't think it'd take much to open it."

Mike said, "That would be breaking and entering. Don't do it."

Emily went around the back. "I have a small view here." The others came over and took turns peeking in. "It looks like no one's been here in ages, just like Ron said."

Henry looked across the property. "I don't see a place to park a boat, do you?"

"No," said Emily. "I think this is a dead end."

Henry tossed the ball for Spunky. "Let's head back before it gets dark. We have to return the boat before the office closes." Spunky ran after the ball, then started barking. Henry called to him. "Come on, boy. Bring back the ball. You know how this works." Spunky continued barking.

Emily said, "Maybe the ball got caught and he can't get at it."

Henry said, "I'll be right back." He ran into the woods. Spunky was standing in front of a brown log cabin with green shudders, camouflaged by the greenery of the woods. It was larger than Barb Rainer's fishing shack. The windows were grime free. Matching curtains hung from the inside. "Come here!" he cried.

Susan, Mike, and Emily ran over. "Did you find the ball?" asked Emily.

"No, but look."

"Another fishing shack?" asked Susan.

"I wouldn't call it a shack. This one's more like a cabin," said Henry.

Emily said, "Do you think someone is living in there?"

Henry said, "Could be."

"I'll bet Ron didn't see this place. We didn't, until Spunky alerted us. It's well hidden by the trees," said Emily. She went to the door and knocked. "No one's answering."

Susan peered through the windows. "Someone *is* staying here. I see a loaf of bread on the counter and a basket of folded laundry on the floor."

Emily knocked again. "Maybe they're out doing errands."

"Or they just use it on weekends," offered Mike.

"It is the weekend," said Susan.

Mike walked around the perimeter of the cabin. "Over in back. Behind the pine trees. Is that a garage?"

"Looks like it," said Henry. He moved closer to it and pressed his nose against one of the tiny square windows. "There's a boat in there."

"I'll bet it's the missing boat!" said Susan.

"Hang on," said Henry. "I imagine most people living this close to the water would own a boat. In any case, this isn't Barb

Rainer's property."

Susan peered into the window. "The detective should see this."

"I'll call Ron," said Henry.

Emily said, "Be sure to tell him we only looked. We didn't open the garage or try to get inside the cabin. I suppose technically we are trespassing."

Henry looked at his watch. "We'd better get moving if we're going to make it back in time to return the boat. I don't want to get stuck paying for an extra day." He started back to the boat. Spunky barked.

"Now what, boy?" said Henry. "I've got your ball, don't worry. Stop pulling on your leash."

Susan's neck hair tingled. She heard rustling. She saw movement. "Someone's watching us! Look by the trees."

"I don't see anyone," said Emily.

"Me neither," said Mike.

I'll bet it was the wind." Henry started the engine. The water splashed against the boat. Susan's hair blew into her face. *There is a breeze. Maybe Henry's right.*

They made it back to the rental office just before sundown.

Emily said to the owner," Do you know who lives in the cabins on Fisherman's Cove?"

"Those properties have been passed down for generations. The younger generation is terrible about upkeep. They're abandoned most of the year." He took the life jackets and gave Henry back his deposit.

By the time they finished chatting, it was dark. They got back into Henry's Jeep and drove away from the pier. Streetlights were sparse—nearly nonexistent. Henry said, "Who's up for a game of Scrabble when we get back to the house?"

"I am," said Susan. "We can finish off that bottle of wine."

"We have enough trouble beating you when we're sober, Susan." Henry swerved.

"Henry, what's going on?" shouted Emily.

"I...I can't see."

Emily grabbed the steering wheel. Bright headlights flooded the Jeep through the back window.

Susan twisted around to look out the back. "It's a car. He's following us."

Henry said, "He's right on my tail." He gripped the steering wheel harder next to Emily's clenched hands. "Bet it's a drunk driver."

"Pull over, Henry. Let him pass," said Emily. Sweat formed on her brow.

"Pull over where? There's practically no shoulder."

"We're coming up on the bridge!" said Emily.

"If you stop now, he'll crash right into us," said Mike. "He's slowing down."

Henry floored the gas. Emily released her grip. Henry peeked in the rearview mirror and eased up. "I think he's gone."

Mike screamed, "Watch out! Here he comes again."

"What kind of sick game is he playing?" said Susan. The hair on her arms stood on end.

"Whatever it is, it's too late to turn back. Brace yourselves. Coming up on the bridge." He pulled into the covered bridge. The car chasing him turned off its headlights. Susan grasped Mike's hand. Her heart pounded in her chest and she felt Mike's hand sweating. The Jeep clunked over the wooden slats.

"Slow and steady," said Emily. If he hits us, it'll be better if we're not going fast."

"But he's racing," said Henry. "He'll slam into us." His hands gripped the steering wheel. "We're almost out of here. Hang on tight." Henry floored the Jeep. Emily gripped his arm. They were out of the bridge. Henry looked in the rear view mirror. "Where did he go?"

Susan and Mike turned around and looked over their shoulders from the back seat. Susan said, "I don't see him. He must still be inside the bridge."

Emily said, "I'll call the police. Let's get out of here."

# Chapter 10

Emily tossed and turned, unable to settle down after nearly being chased off the road. In the morning, Rebecca called.

"Emily, just wanted to let you know I checked the Etsy records and Barb Rainer sold exactly zero of the hair clips you asked about. She sold a handful of scarves and a few pairs of earrings since she put up her e-store, but that's it."

"Thanks, Rebecca. Can you do me another favor, if you're up to it?"

"Tell me what it is, first."

"Yesterday, we discovered another cabin not far from the one that belongs to Barb Rainer. We spotted a boat through the garage window. It's a longshot, but maybe it's the missing boat. Can you find out who owns and/or rents the cabin?"

"I'll try. Fisherman's Cove, right? Send the info and I'll look into it."

Henry, toweling off his hair, emerged from the bathroom. "Who was that?"

"Rebecca. I asked her to look into the cabin we found last night."

"Don't be disappointed if it's not the missing boat. I'll bet everyone on the cove has one." Henry's phone buzzed. "Hey, Ron. Did you figure out who almost ran us off the road last night?"

"Not yet. That road is pretty much deserted after dark and we don't have any CCTV out there. We're working on it. Whoever chased you was trying to scare you off and he'll only escalate if you keep prying."

"I know, but we must be onto something or why would he bother?"

"I'll keep you posted," said Ron. "There's still a chance it was a drunk fisherman or a couple of teenagers out joy riding."

He and Emily climbed down the ladder into the living room. Susan and Mike were already up and dressed.

Susan said, "Have you heard back from the police?"

"Yeah, nothing yet. Just a warning to stay clear."

"What are we doing today?" asked Susan.

"There's an arts festival at St. Edwards College," said Emily. "We're on fall break this week so they opened up the library to local artists."

Susan said, "That sounds like fun."

Emily said, "It doesn't open until one. Let's take a drive and have lunch somewhere before then."

"A drive, to the boat rental office? And to the cove where we saw the second cabin?" asked Henry. "Ron warned us to keep away." Emily didn't respond.

After breakfast, they drove around looking at autumn foliage and as predicted, wound up renting a boat and heading back to Fisherman's Cove.

Susan zipped her jacket to the chin. The weather had turned

cooler overnight. She thought back to yesterday. She knew she'd seen movement in the trees. She knew she'd heard rustling. Good Lord, the dog even heard it. He barked to get Henry's attention, but Henry ignored him.

Susan said, "You don't think the incident on the bridge was a coincidence, do you?"

"No," said Henry.

"You all didn't believe me when I said someone was behind the pine trees. I think whoever it was followed us and tried to run us off the road."

Mike said, "We didn't see any other boats on the way back. No one crossed the lake."

Emily said, "You can get to the pier by taking the back road. It isn't paved, but it's serviceable. They must have figured we'd stop at the boat rental office."

"And they followed us when we finished," said Susan. "I'm sure of it."

"Maybe we should turn around and go home," said Henry. "Ron is right. We shouldn't be poking around risking our lives."

"Stop being so dramatic," said Emily. "It's broad daylight and there are four of us. We'll be okay."

Henry pulled the boat next to the pier and Mike helped secure it.

Henry led them past Barb's cabin to the second cabin they'd discovered.

"The lights are on," said Susan. Excitement crept through her body. "Someone's inside. Let's knock."

"No," said Henry. "It's not a good..." The front door opened, and a woman stepped out. She looked to be around forty, with a chic haircut and designer jeans. She was accompanied by a black lab on a leash.

"Get down," whispered Henry.

Susan whispered, "Now's our chance." She walked toward the cabin.

The woman took a step back when she saw them. Susan waved to her. "Hello. That's a beautiful dog you've got. What's its name?"

"Um, Oreo."

"Because of the white under his chin, right?

"Because the day I brought him home, he tore into a package of Oreos. Good thing I stopped him before he made himself sick. Who are you people?"

"I'm Susan. This is my husband Mike. That's Henry and Emily."

Emily said, "We live on the other side of Lake Pleasant. Our friends here are visiting from New York. We're just showing them around."

"I'm Patrice." She zipped her jacket, maneuvering around the leash.

Susan bent down to pet Oreo. "Quiet out here, isn't it? Bet you don't have to worry about noisy neighbors."

Mike said, "We passed one other cabin on the way in from the shore. It looks sort of deserted."

"Yeah, I haven't seen any signs of life," said Patrice.

Susan stood back up. "What happens if there's an emergency? I mean, can an ambulance or the police get here in a reasonable amount of time? For example, did you hear about the man who drowned across the lake? Bad enough no one heard or saw it before it was too late, but imagine being all the way out here?"

"It hasn't been a problem."

"I bet it's a problem in the winter when the lake freezes. Do you stay here through the winter? Mike is about to retire and I'm loving the idea of a lakeside cabin when he does. I suppose you'd need a boat, right?"

"It's not an island. There's a road leading into town. I myself don't own a boat. And I haven't left this place for weeks." Oreo's leash jangled. "He's anxious to start his walk. Enjoy your visit."

"Wait," said Susan. "The night the man was murdered, did you see or hear anything unusual?"

"From here? No. I'm way too far from Pier 12 to have heard anything." Oreo tugged her along.

Emily said, "She doesn't know anything. This was a waste of time as far as information gathering goes."

Susan said, "Not so fast. Did the police say where the body was found? When I heard the local news, they didn't mention a location. And even if they said 'the pier,' how would she know which pier if she saw nothing?"

Mike said, "Guess that boat in the garage doesn't belong to her."

Henry said, "Is she gone?"

"Yeah," said Mike.

"One more thing." He checked to make sure the coast was clear, then scooted over to the garage window and took a picture of the boat. "Let's go."

Emily said, "Wait. Look at the car. A silver BMW. Expensive. You think she could afford a nicer cabin."

Susan bent down and examined the tires. "There are pieces of gravel stuck in the treads. Wasn't the road we took to the bridge last night covered in gravel?"

Emily said, "Yes, I thought Henry was going to wind up with a flat."

Mike said, "There are tire tracks leading around back. Is that where the road is located?"

"I think so," said Henry. "And it rained the day Mike and

Susan arrived. Five days ago. Tire treads that had been here for weeks would have washed away by now. She lied to us."

# Chapter 11

After a leisurely lunch, they headed to the campus. St. Edwards, where Emily taught part-time, was a small liberal arts college nestled in the mountains. Even with the students on fall break, parking was a nightmare. Luckily, Emily remembered to transfer her faculty parking tag to the Jeep and they were able to park near the library.

Emily said, "They have an outdoors arts festival here in the spring when the weather is warmer. It includes performing arts, so you get to see students acting, playing music, and singing in addition to displaying their artwork."

Henry said, "I keep thinking I'd like to sell some of my handmade furniture pieces."

"Why?" said Emily. "It's not like we need the money."

"Have you looked at college tuitions lately?"

She cleared her throat. "Have you forgotten I work at a college? And we'd get a tuition break if she goes here."

"No offense, but Maddy wants to go to vet school. A small liberal arts college won't work for her."

They entered the main library, with its British village charm and its aroma of worn books mingled with the fresh scent of new releases. The artists were set up around the perimeter.

Susan said, "Look! Handmade jewelry." She ran over to the first booth and held a pair of glass earrings up to the light.

"Those are cute," said Emily. She rummaged through a rack of bangle bracelets. "What do you think of the trend of wearing an armful of bracelets?"

Susan said, "More than one on my wrist, two at the most, is all I can tolerate."

Henry said, "Em, don't look now, but isn't that Barb Rainer behind the next table?"

Emily turned around slowly. "It sure is. She has an Etsy shop, so it's not surprising she's here at a local event."

Susan said, "Look who she's talking to! Isn't that the woman we just saw at the cabin at the cove?"

"Patrice!" said Emily. "She didn't waste any time getting here."

Henry put his hand on Emily's shoulder. "She could be browsing just like we are."

"Patrice is showing Barb something on her phone."

Mike said, "A piece she saw in the Etsy shop, perhaps?"

"I suppose it shouldn't be a surprise they know each other," said Susan. "After all, they're neighbors out on the cove."

"But Barb said she hasn't been out there in ages," said Emily. "And Patrice acted as though she had no idea who owns Barb's cabin."

Henry said, "Barb and Patrice are looking at us. Come on, let's go say hello."

Emily led the way. "Barb, I'm glad to see you out and about after all you're dealing with."

"Gotta earn a living somehow. Gotta pay that second mortgage that was dumped on me. Oh, and apparently he had a gambling debt I knew nothing about. Lord knows that ain't my problem. I told the goon who showed up at my door looking for him he'd have an easier time getting blood from a rock."

"Gambling debt? Do you think it's a motive?" asked Emily.

Barb shrugged her shoulders. "Beats me."

Susan said, "Hi, Patrice. I didn't know you and Barb knew each other."

"We don't," said Patrice. "We were just discussing bracelets. I saw one I liked on her Etsy site."

"Do you know the two of you are neighbors?" asked Susan.

"No, we're not," said Barb. I know my neighbors on either side of my farm, and my back fence neighbors, too. Patrice isn't one of them."

Susan continued. "I meant out on the cove. The fishing cabin that you inherited is practically next door to Patrice's cabin."

Barb fidgeted. "I told you I haven't been out there in over a decade. If we're neighbors, it's news to me."

Patrice nodded. "I told you I haven't seen anyone there."

Susan said, "Patrice, did you inherit your cabin as well? For all you know, your parents and Barb's may have been friends."

"I didn't inherit anything. My parents are still alive. I'm just renting," said Patrice.

"Renting? From who?" asked Susan. "Like I said, Mike and I might be interested in getting our own cabin."

"I'd have to look for her card. I walked into an office downtown and walked out with a set of keys and a lease."

"Downtown?" asked Susan. "Near which shop?"

"I don't remember," said Patrice.

Emily said, "Was it the one by the comic book store?"

"Yes, that was it."

"Are you originally from Vermont?" asked Emily.

"No. Now, I'd like to continue with my shopping." She started walking away.

Barb said, "Wait, don't you want to see the matching earrings?"

Patrice shook her head and continued walking away.

"You just lost me a sale," said Barb. "If you're not buying, move along to make room for those who are here to shop."

Susan opened her purse and dug into her wallet. "I'll take this whole set. Earrings, bracelet, and pendant. What do I owe you?"

"Forty dollars for the set," said Barb.

Henry said, "Barb, you should tell the police about the goon who showed up at your door. You never know, it could be a lead."

"Yeah. I was going to call them anyway to see when they'll release Chet's body so I can be done with him for good."

Susan took the wrapped jewelry from Barb. "I can always order more online, right?"

"Yep." Barb turned her attention to a couple combing through the hair ornaments. Susan, Mike, Emily, and Henry continued down the aisle.

Emily said, "Patrice is hiding something."

"What do you mean?" asked Susan.

"The comic book store closed shortly after Henry and I moved here. If Patrice arrived here when she said she did, she'd never have known there was such a store."

They continued past the various booths. Patrice was behind a divider, on her phone. While the others browsed the used books table, Susan put her ear against the divider.

Patrice whispered into the phone. "We've got to lay low. I think it's time for me to disappear before the police or the nosy tourist and company put it together. No. It's in my garage and has to be dealt with. Tomorrow night? I'll come over tonight and we can discuss it. No, at the farm. Later."

Emily tapped Susan on the shoulder. "What's so interesting?"

"I just overheard Patrice on the phone. She's meeting someone at the farm tonight. Barb, I'll bet."

"Barb's booth is buzzing. Look. I doubt she was talking on the phone with so many customers there. She's not the only one in town who lives on a farm."

"Then who was she talking to?"

Henry came over. "They've got funnel cakes around the corner. Just saying."

Around the corner, the aroma wouldn't allow them to escape if they wanted to. And they didn't. They bought funnel cakes and sat at a table in the make-shift café area.

Emily said, "Why don't we head downtown after we finish here."

"Excellent," said Susan. "I want to go back to the baby clothing store and pick up a few more things."

"Sure," said Mike. "And while we're there, stop by the real estate office, right? You can't fool me."

"Two birds, one stone," said Susan.

Henry said, "Mike and I have had enough wandering through craft fairs and shops. How about you two go downtown, and I'll take Mike bowling, or to the sports bar."

"No objection here," said Emily.

"Then, it's settled. We'll see you back at the house at dinner time."

# Chapter 12

Mike and Henry spent a couple of hours at the bowling alley. Mike, who hadn't mentioned he was on a championship-winning bowling team back in Westbrook, clobbered Henry, who wasn't accustomed to losing in anything.

"One more game?" asked Mike.

"Are you kidding? My ego can't take it."

"And that was without my custom bowling ball and lucky shoes. Did you say something about a sports bar? Come on, I'm buying."

They hopped in the Jeep, and drove to a sports bar sandwiched between a newly built Applebee's and a vintage movie theater.

Inside, sports reruns played on the TVs and beer was 'buy one get one free.' Happy Hour had begun. Henry and Mike squeezed into a booth.

Henry said, "The local craft beers are pretty good." He pointed to an item on the menu. "I've had this one before."

"Want to split an appetizer?" said Mike. "Since my heart surgery, Susan is on me all the time about what I eat. I wouldn't mind an order of sliders and onion rings."

"Deal," said Henry.

The waiter came by for their order. "Who are you going for in the big game tonight?"

Henry said, "Rangers."

"Not me," said the waiter. "Boston Bruins all the way. What about you? Are you going for the winning team?"

"I'm from New York," said Mike. "Rangers all the way."

"Bets are closing soon. If you want in, Pug is collecting until six." He pointed to a thin guy with a ponytail. "Be right back with your beer."

Mike said, "I thought gambling was illegal in this state."

"So did I," said Henry.

"Do you suppose the gambling debt Barb mentioned had to do with sports betting?"

"Your guess is as good as mine." Henry watched as a man entered the bar and made a beeline to Pug. The man said something hard to hear over the TV, and counted out a handful of bills which Pug took and stuck in his pocket. Then, the man walked out without sitting or ordering a drink.

The waiter brought the beer to the table. "Lotta dough to be made tonight. The Rangers are the underdog. Just saying."

"Do you have to pay ahead?" asked Henry.

"New customers, yes. Loyal clients like myself, we can call it in and owe him later."

"What happens if someone places a bet and doesn't pay up?" asked Mike.

"You've seen the movies, right? Let's just say there have been rumors of broken legs and concussions. See the two men sitting across the booth from Pug?"

"They could do serious damage judging by the size of their

arms," said Mike.

"Ex Marines. They work for Pug. A word of advice. It's a bad idea to welch on a bet. I'll be back with your sliders."

Meanwhile, Susan and Emily spent the afternoon downtown. They strolled past the bookstore and bakery.

Emily said, "The old comic book store was right past the bank. Come on. Here. Now it's a souvenir shop."

"There's the real estate office," said Susan. "Come on." She opened the door which triggered a bell announcing their arrival.

A middle-aged woman with a loose bun and expertly applied makeup greeted them. "Can I help you?"

Susan said, "I hope so. My husband and I are thinking of retiring and moving up here. Someone mentioned they found their rental through your office."

"What area are we talking about?" said the realtor.

"Fisherman's Cove," said Emily.

"Quiet area. Have a seat." She pulled a second chair in front of her desk. "Can I get you coffee or water?"

"No, thanks," said Susan. Emily shook her head.

"There's a new rental community on the east side of the lake, north of Fisherman's Cove," said the realtor.

"I had my heart set on the cove itself," said Susan.

"Rentals are scare if not non-existent out there. There are only a handful of properties and they tend to stay in the families for generations."

"Surely some family members don't live in the area. Don't they rent the properties out?"

The woman clicked the keys on her computer. "There aren't any properties for rent in that area."

"Can I get on a waiting list?" said Susan.

"I mean, there are no rentals, period. Just as I thought. "You'd be better off in the newer units, in any case."

"Our friend rents a cabin next to an old fishing cottage." Susan walked around the desk, pushed up her bifocals, and looked at the map on the computer screen. "There. That's where she's living."

The realtor clicked the keys. "Oh, that property belongs to Theo and Margie Amos."

"And a Patrice…Amos?" said Susan.

"No Patrice. I know this couple from church. They're elderly, sweet as can be. No kids, just cats. They head down to Florida every winter. Come back around Easter time. Margie showed up to church in an old-fashioned Easter bonnet last year. Looked like that lady in the margarine commercial. Blue bonnet. Only hers was white with a big fabric daisy attached to the ribbon. I've mentioned to them that they should rent the place out while they're gone, but they don't want the hassle and risk of damage. Besides, truthfully, no one rents a place for the winter in Sugarbury Falls."

"I thought skiing was big here," said Susan.

"There are tons of short term rentals and Airbnbs much closer to the slopes. If I could escape the winter weather, I'd fly down to Florida myself before the snow starts up."

Emily said, "You don't happen to know if they own a boat, do you?"

"A boat? I can't imagine them getting in and out of a boat. Theo's using a walker these days."

"Thanks for your time," said Susan.

"Wait! Don't you want to consider the places that are available?"

"I'll talk it over with my husband and get back to you," said Susan.

Outside, Susan said, "How is Patrice renting if the Amoses

don't rent the place?"

"I wonder if she's squatting. You know, like she just saw it empty and moved in."

Susan said, "She certainly seems to have the money to rent or buy a place of her own."

"The realtor said there are no rentals available."

"But why didn't she go up the road and get one of the new places?" asked Susan.

Emily shrugged. "Let's go. I was thinking dinner at Coralee's would be nice tonight,"

When they got home, Mike and Henry were already back.

Mike said, "Henry was just showing me his woodworking studio. They converted the old barn."

"I remember," said Susan. "Did you have fun bowling?"

"I did," said Mike. "I'm not too sure about Henry. I made it up to him. We went to a sports bar and had a couple of beers."

Emily said, "Henry hates losing. No matter what it is."

Henry said, "We stumbled upon an illegal sports betting operation at the bar. A guy named Pug and his two bouncers."

"Pug?" said Emily. "You're making this up."

"No, seriously," said Henry. "Didn't Barb say Chet had gambling debt?"

"She did," said Emily. "Do you think Chet owed money to Pug and he had his bouncers off him?"

Henry said, "I don't know. And I don't want to mention this to Ron."

"Why not?" said Emily. "It could be a lead."

"Think about it. The betting operation gets raided. The waiter at the bar tells the cops about two men he hadn't seen before coming into the bar and nosing around about illegal betting. They access the CCTV and voila. Mike and I are next on the hit list."

"You've got a point," said Emily. "It's probably unrelated, anyhow. We heard gambling debt. That could mean anything from a poker game to horse races. There's nothing tying Chet to Pug. And, I can't ask Rebecca to get background information knowing only the name Pug. She's good, but really?"

Maddy came in with Spunky and took off his leash. Spunky trotted over to his water bowl. "Brooke asked me to come over for dinner and study together for a test. Is that okay?"

Emily said, "We're going to Coralee's for dinner. It's up to you."

"I should go study. Can you bring me back dessert?"

"Will do," said Emily. She scooped Chester off the back of the sofa. "It's been a full day. Let's go to dinner before I fall asleep," said Emily. She was glad she was on fall break and didn't have to grade stories or get up early to teach class.

# Chapter 13

Coralee greeted them in the lobby. "I saved you the table overlooking the golf course."

"Looks busy tonight, thanks," said Emily. "I smell garlic. Did you make your pasta with garlic and oil?"

"I sure did."

She and the others followed Coralee to the table. "Coralee, do you know a Theo and Marge Amos?"

"Sure. Always ate brunch here after church on Sundays. They go south for the winters. Why?"

"We spoke to a realtor, who said they never rent their cabin out on Fisherman's Cove when they go away for the winter, but we know a woman named Patrice has been living there."

"Patrice who?" asked Coralee.

"Don't know her last name. We ran into her at the cove, and again at the St. Edward's craft fair earlier today."

"The only Patrice I know rents half a duplex from my friend Cybil across the bridge."

Emily said, "Must not be her. Why would you rent a cabin ten minutes away from your home?"

"What does she look like?" asked Coralee. "You never know."

"Chicly-cut reddish brown hair with a blond streak. Fortyish, slim."

"Sure sounds like the same Patrice."

"Do you think she's a friend of the Amoses?" asked Emily. "Maybe they asked her to keep an eye on the place. She had a dog with her. Maybe she's pet sitting."

"No, I'm sure they don't have a dog, and they're funny about having anyone stay in their home. They were friendly with the neighbors before they died. Maybe Barb Rainer knows something. You should ask her."

"I heard she doesn't go out to the family cabin," said Emily.

"Of course, she does, to check on it. In fact, she even asked me if I knew a good plumber because a pipe rusted through."

"When?" asked Emily.

"A few weeks back." Coralee scanned the crowded dining room. "The specials tonight are pasta with garlic and oil, of course, vegetable lasagna with lemon braised asparagus tips, and grilled seabass with fingerling potatoes. I'll tell the server you're here."

"Seabass sounds good to me," said Henry. The server took their orders and brought them drinks.

Emily said, "If it's the same Patrice who rents from Coralee's friend, what's she doing living at the cove?"

Henry said, "A busted pipe. Paint fumes. Any number of reasons. Em, let's give it a rest and enjoy our dinner." He picked up his wine glass. "To old friends. The best kind."

They lingered over the meal, then ordered the pumpkin cheesecake for dessert. Coralee packed one to go for Maddy.

In the parking lot, Susan spotted Kirby. She called to her, but the woman was too far away to hear. They saw her get into the passenger side of a black truck. "That's Kirby Taylor, isn't it?"

Emily said, "Yes, it is."

"I wonder where she's going?" said Susan. "And who's behind the wheel."

"I'm surprised she's still here," said Mike. "Haven't they released the body yet? Who pays for the funeral? Do you think they'll split the cost?"

Susan said, "At the arts fair, I overheard Patrice arranging to meet someone at a farm. "Who do we know that has a farm?"

Emily said, "Barb Rainer."

"Want to swing by Barb's place and see if she's there?"

"What are we going to do, knock and ask them why they're meeting?" asked Mike.

Susan said, "We won't let them know we're there. We'll keep our distance."

"We observe from a distance," said Henry. "We stay in the car, drive by, and see if we spot a silver BMW. Then, we go home."

"It's a deal." Susan reached over and shook his hand.

"I'll bring my binoculars," said Henry.

They relaxed the rest of the day. After dinner, they drove through the donut shop drive-thru, continued to Barb Rainer's farm, and parked behind the barn where they had a clear view of her driveway. A black Ford pick-up truck was parked in the driveway.

Susan said, "That truck looks familiar."

"Rebecca told us Barb drives a black Ford pick-up truck," said Emily.

"There are plenty of black pickup trucks around here," said Henry. He picked up the binoculars. "Looks like she's making dinner."

"Let me have a look," said Emily. Henry handed her the

binoculars.

"Told you, she's just making dinner," said Henry. "Let me have those back."

"Now, what's she doing?" asked Susan.

"Eating and reading the newspaper," said Henry. "She's up. She's moving. I think she just went into the bathroom."

"Thrilling," said Mike. "Can you pass the Munchkins?"

Susan said, "Where did I see that truck? It's bugging me."

"Probably parked at the arts fair," said Henry. "She's coming out of the bathroom. Now, she's making coffee."

"We've been here an hour," said Mike. "How much longer do you want to wait? The Rangers are playing tonight. It's televised. They're playing the Bruins."

"She just turned off the kitchen light. Another light went on. She's in the living room."

"Can you see anything?" asked Emily.

"She turned on the TV. She's relaxing on the sofa," said Henry.

"Let me have another turn with the binoculars," said Emily. Henry handed them over.

"Look!" said Susan. "Headlights."

Emily aimed the binoculars toward the road. "It's a car. It's slowing down."

"It's pulling into the driveway," said Mike. "Don't need binoculars to see that."

Emily said, "It's a Silver BMW! That's Patrice's car."

"We thought as much. The question is why is she here?" Susan grabbed a donut from the bag of Munchkins they'd picked up on the way.

Henry took back the binoculars. "She's getting out of the car. She's wearing a parka. Didn't someone mention a woman in a parka? Was it the boat rental guy?"

Emily said, "She's knocking. There. Barb is letting her in. Can you see through the window, Henry?"

"Yeah. She's taking Patrice's coat. Kitchen light is on again. She's pouring coffee. Two mugs."

"If the coffee was already made, it means she was expecting company," said Susan. She licked powdered sugar off her fingers.

Henry refocused the binoculars. "They're sitting on the sofa. Patrice just pulled a legal pad out of her mega purse. She's drawing or writing something. Barb put on her reading glasses. She's nodding."

"I'd love to be a fly on the wall," said Susan.

Henry said, "They're huddled over the paper. Barb's getting up. She's going to the desk. She's picking up a packet of some kind. Patrice is signing it."

"What do you suppose she's signing?" asked Emily. "Do you think the Amoses changed their mind and Barb rented out the cabin for them?"

"Maybe the Amoses don't know she's renting out their cabin. Barb said she needs money," said Mike. "She has an emergency key, and she knows the Amoses won't be back until spring."

"Maybe she's buying more of that Etsy stuff," said Mike. "She's filling out an order form or something."

Henry refocused the binoculars. "I don't see jewelry or barrettes anywhere."

Mike said, "We found out what we came for. Barb and Patrice know each other. Can we go now?"

Susan said, "I kind of have to pee."

Henry put the binoculars back in their case and started the Jeep.

# Chapter 14

Over breakfast the next morning, Emily said, "Kirby and Barb must be curious about each other after learning they shared a husband."

Susan said, "Imagine if they start comparing notes? I'm sure they'd have lots to talk about."

"I couldn't sleep trying to figure out why Patrice is living on the cove," said Emily.

Susan said, "It doesn't make sense. We could check out her duplex."

Emily said, "I've got Patrice's address. Rebecca gave it to me. Anyone want more coffee or scrambled eggs?"

"I'll take more coffee," said Mike. He handed Spunky a bit of scrambled egg under the table.

When they'd finished, Susan and Emily headed to the inn. Kirby was sitting on the porch, bundled in a blanket, reading a book. She looked up at them. "Are you here for breakfast? Coralee made the most delicious quiche."

"No," said Emily. "We came to see how you're holding up."

Susan said, "Is the baby doing okay?"

"The baby is fine. I'm still processing all of this. One day at a time."

Emily said, "When you get back home, I'm sure you can find a support group. It might help to be with others going through what you're going through."

"Other people who've lost someone they loved, then found out they didn't know that person at all? Other people whose life with their loved one was a total sham?"

"Have you met Barb Rainer?" asked Emily. "This must be so hard on both of you."

"Who?" asked Kirby.

"The other wife," said Emily. "She'd understand."

"Barb Rainer. So that's her name. I never met her. I suppose when the body is finally released, we might need to talk. I highly doubt there's a will to worry about. Denver blew all his money on gambling."

"Gambling?" said Susan. "Isn't it illegal in Vermont?"

"So is marrying more than one wife and stealing identities. You think that stopped him?"

"You have a point. His death could be related to his gambling. Do you know what type of gambling he was involved in?" asked Emily.

"Poker, mostly. He wasn't very good at it either, though he sure managed the poker face when hiding where he'd been on his business trips."

"We saw you leave with someone in a black truck," said Susan. "When we checked the CCTV with Coralee. It looked like Barb Rainer's truck."

"Black pickup truck? Barb Rainer? That wasn't me. I don't know anyone in this town outside of the two of you and Coralee. I just want to get back home and plan for this baby." She shuddered. "I'm getting cold. I'm going back inside."

After she went in, Susan said, "I'm not crazy. I saw her get into Barb Rainer's truck. Why is she lying?"

"I don't know," said Emily.

"Where's that address you got from Rebecca?" asked Susan.

"Patrice's?" Emily found it on her phone. "Want to swing by?"

"Sure."

They drove across town, past St. Edwards College. "It's number 1011," said Emily.

Susan peered out the passenger side window. "Right there. The brick duplex. Is it A or B?"

"Rebecca didn't say. Guess we can knock and find out." Emily pulled into the driveway. "I don't see a silver BMW."

"She's probably still out on Fisherman's Cove. Come on. If we don't find her, the neighbor might know something."

They knocked on side A and an elderly woman in a terry cloth sweat suit opened the door. It smelled vaguely like a litter box. "Can I help you?"

Emily said, "Sorry to bother you. We're looking for your neighbor, Patrice. We weren't sure which side of the duplex she was on."

"Come in before the cold air gets in. Heating bill is so expensive come winter." A cat jumped off the back of the sofa. "Patrice is gone. Didn't say a word, just disappeared. Haven't seen her or her husband in over a week."

"Her husband?" asked Emily.

"Yeah. Blake."

"Maybe they're on vacation?" said Susan. "What makes you think they're gone for good?"

"She left the keys and the last rent check in my mailbox. I own this place. I live here and rent the other side. She left me with no warning. Not the best time of year to get renters."

Emily said, "You had no idea she was leaving? And you say she's married?"

"They were practically newlyweds. He moved in with her a couple of months ago fresh from their honeymoon. They left their stuff and everything. Must have been in a big hurry."

"I know this is awkward, but can we see the place?" asked Susan. "My husband and I, we're from New York. We're thinking of retiring here. After all, our oldest and dearest friends live here." She put her arm around Emily.

"Why not? I need to get it rented. It's a lovely place. Mirror image of my place. I put in new carpeting right before Patrice moved in." She grabbed the keys. "Let's go."

The door opened into a small foyer and faced a staircase. A living room with a leather sofa, wall-mounted TV, and recliner was to the right. To the left, a dining room with an island separating it from the kitchen.

"Spacious," said Susan. "Can we see upstairs?"

"Yeah. It's two bedrooms with a tub and shower in the master suite. There's a bathroom with a shower only that you can access either from the hallway, or from the second bedroom."

Susan opened the closet in the master bedroom. An empty bar full of bare hangers. She opened the drawers which were likewise, empty. "They took the time to pack their clothes," said Susan.

"They left a bunch of papers in the second bedroom. They used it as an office, though I don't know why they needed an office. He was always away on business, and she came and went regular work hours."

Susan walked out of the room and into the second bedroom. "They did leave a mess in here. Took the time to pack up their computer, I see." She picked up dangling computer cables hanging out of the wall. The woman's phone rang.

"Oh, it's the realtor. I'm listing this place, so if you want it, you should tell me before the listing goes up. I'll be right back. I've got to take this."

She went down the stairs, shoes tapping against the varnished steps.

"Husband?" whispered Emily. "We didn't see a husband at the cabin and there was only the silver BMW parked in the driveway."

"Let's see if she left anything interesting behind." Susan flipped through the papers on the desk. She noticed wadded up receipts in the trash basket and rummaged through them.

"What are you doing going through that filthy trash?" said Emily.

"Only paper in here." She kept unfolding wadded bits of paper. She opened a receipt and her heart fluttered. "Oh, my."

"What? What's that?"

"You'll like this. Here's a receipt for a boat rental. It's dated the 29th. That's the day before we discovered the body."

"Oh, my God. *She* rented the boat. She could be the killer."

Emily said, "What's *her* connection to Chet/Denver?"

"Hopefully she wasn't married to him," said Susan. She flipped through a stack of papers.

Susan peeked out the doorway. "She's still gabbing to the real estate agent." She stopped and pulled out a spread sheet. "Emily, look at this. It's a grid of sports teams and dates. There's a column for money, and names written on the side."

"Like a gambling coordinator might use? Do you think…"

"That Pug could be her husband and Patrice helped him kill Chet/Denver when he didn't pay his debts?" asked Susan. "Do you think they skipped town?"

"I think she's still at Fisherman's Cove," said Emily. "I don't know where he's hiding. I hear footsteps. Quick, put that trash back in the basket. She must be off the phone."

The woman came back into the room. "What do you think of the place?"

Susan said, "It's great. Let me take one last look around downstairs." She wandered back into the living room. "Let me speak to my husband and get back to you."

While Susan and Emily checked out Patrice's duplex, Henry and Mike rented a boat at the pier.

Henry said, "Couldn't let you come all the way up here and not go fishing. I'm of the catch and release school. Emily and Maddy would kill me if I came home with a fish. They're both vegetarians and animal advocates."

"I hear you. I like being out on the water." Mike grabbed a beer from the cooler. They rowed toward the other side of the lake.

Henry paddled around a bend. "This is an untapped reservoir. Most people don't know about it. I caught half a dozen fish last time I was out here."

Henry pulled out his bait. "I even use fake worms."

Mike picked up his reel and cast it out. "Are you sure there are fish in here?"

Henry cast his reel and they waited. And waited. Henry said, "Let's row a little closer to shore." He cast out his line.

Mike said, "My hook is stuck on something and I don't think it's a fish."

"You must have caught it in the rocks. Let's get closer and try to unravel it." He paddled toward the shore.

Mike said, "I'm afraid the line's going to snap." They paddled over. He pulled low-hanging vines off the top. "It's a hunk of metal. I think it's a motor."

Henry reached down. "A motor like the one on our boat. It's not rusted. Couldn't have been here for long."

"Do you think it's from the missing boat?" asked Mike. "I'll call the police."

"No cell service out here. We're close to Fisherman's Cove. Before we bother the police, let's see if the boat's still in that garage."

"What are we waiting for?" asked Mike.

No longer concerned about staying quiet for the sake of catching fish, Henry started the motor and they docked their boat at the rickety pier at Fisherman's Cove. They followed the path to the cabin.

"I don't see a car in the driveway," said Henry.

Mike peered through the window. "No one's home. There's a full trash bag on the kitchen floor. Think Patrice left?"

"Don't know. Maybe the girls found her at her place in town." He jogged over to the garage and peered into the window. "The boat is gone!"

# Chapter 15

Back in the Jeep heading home, Mike called Ron at the station. Ron promised he'd get right on it. When they got home, the girls were relaxing in the living room.

Emily hopped up. "You won't believe what we found out! Patrice was married. They were renting a duplex, then took off in a hurry."

"We can top that," said Henry. "We found a boat motor identical to the ones on the rental boats from the fishing shack. Ron's heading over there now. And looks like Patrice deserted the cabin."

"Really?" said Emily. "She ditched the boat?"

"Looks that way," said Henry.

Mike said, "Who was Patrice's husband?"

"I don't know," said Emily. "I have my suspicions. Susan found a spread sheet of sports matches and dates. Something a person gathering bets might use."

"Like Pug," asked Mike. "Did you ask the woman who owned the duplex what Patrice's husband looks like?"

"No, but we can run back over and find out."

Susan said, "Barb and Kirby have alibis for the night of the murder, but we have no idea where Patrice was that night."

Emily grabbed her coat. "Susan and I will check with the duplex owner."

Henry said, "And ask if she remembers seeing them the night of the murder. Mike and I will go back to Coralee's. We looked for a blue car, Kirby's car, leaving the night of the murder. Maybe we should look for a black pickup truck instead." His phone vibrated. "It's Ron."

"Think he traced the motor already?" asked Emily.

Henry answered the call. "Yes, that's it. We saw the motor."

Emily whispered in his ear. "Put it on speaker."

Ron said, "The motor came from the missing boat. Anything else you can tell us?"

"There was a boat parked in the Amos' garage. It's not there now," said Henry.

"My guys found it. Not far from where you found the motor. It's the missing boat."

"Thanks for keeping us in the loop," said Henry. He stuck his phone in his pocket.

"You got all that?"

"Yep. Meet you back here," said Emily. She and Susan took off in Emily's Audi. They zipped across town and knocked on the duplex owner's door.

"Ah," said the owner. She looked directly at Susan. "You decided to take the rental."

Susan said, "This isn't about the rental. In fact, I have to confess. We came to find out about Patrice. We think she may have killed her husband."

"What! You think she killed Blake?" asked the owner.

"Can you describe Patrice's husband?" asked Susan. "Was he

tall and skinny, with long hair?"

"No," said the owner. "He was bald and kind of chunky if you ask me. At his age, he should be watching the fat and calories or he'll wind up like my poor Billy. Dead before his time."

Emily took out her phone. "Is this Blake?" She showed her the photos Rebecca had scrounged up.

"Wait! It's too dark in here." The owner flicked on the lamp.

"Now, can you tell?" asked Emily.

"Hmm. I need my reading glasses. Just a second. Where did I put them?"

"There. On the coffee table," said Susan. She was losing patience.

Emily held the phone up to her nose. "Can you see, now?"

"Yes, that's him. The glasses are different, but it's him."

Emily said, "Do you remember seeing Patrice and Blake the night of the 29th?"

"I can't remember one day from the next." Her gray tabby meowed at her feet.

"It was last week. It stormed later that night."

"Stormed? Ah, yes. I remember. The electric went out and I knocked on their door to borrow a second flashlight. No one was home."

"You're positive?"

"Yes."

"Okay," said Emily. "The police may contact you for more information."

"You think I was renting to a murderer? How could I not have seen it? They were such nice people."

"Ted Bundy was described as the perfect neighbor and he turned out to be a serial killer," said Susan.

Henry explained to Coralee what they needed. She cued up the security footage. "What are we looking for, again?"

Henry said, "We're looking for a Kirby getting into a black pickup truck the night of the 29th."

Coralee started the footage. It rolled into the afternoon. "Nothing, yet."

"Keep going," said Henry.

"What's that?" said Mike. Coralee stopped the tape. "Back it up a little." Mike looked at each frame. "No, it's not a black truck, it's blue. Not the same one."

Coralee rolled through the footage into the evening. "How late do you want to go?" asked Coralee.

"Wait, stop!" said Henry. "Back it up. There. Zoom in. It's Barb's truck."

"Are you sure?" asked Mike.

"Yeah. See. Coralee, go ahead slowly."

Mike said, "Someone's coming out the front. She's getting into the passenger side. Is that Kirby? It's hard to tell with the jacket on."

Henry leaned in. "It's her! Barb picked up Kirby the night of the murder."

Henry headed back to his house with Mike. Emily and Susan were already home. Emily hopped up off the sofa.

"Our hunch was right. Blake, Patrice's husband, also goes by the name Chet Rainer and Denver Taylor."

Henry said, "And we looked at the footage with Coralee. Barb came by and picked up Kirby at the inn the night of the murder."

"You saw Barb and Kirby together in the car?"

Henry said, "We couldn't see Barb, but we assumed since it's her truck, she was driving."

"I called Rebecca," said Emily. "She's on the way over."

Rebecca knocked. "You made progress. Tell me what you need."

"Check out a marriage and driver's license for Blake Higgins," said Emily. "He's married to…was married to…Patrice Higgins."

Rebecca tapped the keys. "Higgins is a common last name."

"They were married recently. Maybe a few months ago."

"Got it. And the driver's license. And guess what?"

"Blake Higgins is an alias also?" asked Susan.

"Yep. Blake Higgins died a decade ago."

Emily said, "Now we know he had at least three identities."

"What about Barb Rainer's alibi? She was at bible study the night you asked about," said Rebecca. "I double checked with Abby and she swears she didn't leave."

"How late does bible study run?" asked Emily.

"Abby's always home before nine."

Henry said, "The footage from Coralee's shows Barb picking up Kirby at the inn just before ten. She finished bible study, maybe went home to change clothes or stopped for a cup of coffee, and then picked up Kirby."

"Patrice couldn't have killed him without help," said Emily. "Someone had to have lured him into the woods and convinced him to go to the pier."

Susan said, "Meanwhile, the boat had to be waiting at the pier, or he wouldn't have died wearing a life jacket."

"Why did they leave him? Why not stick him in the boat and move the body?" asked Mike.

Henry said, "He was a big guy. The four of us struggled to get him out of the water. Maybe they hoped it'd look like an accident, or they were interrupted." He picked up the phone.

"Who are you calling?" asked Emily.

"I'm calling Ron. He has to know Kirby left the inn with Barb the night of the murder. It blows up both of their alibis."

# Chapter 16

Ron stopped by the house later that evening. "All three of the wives are gone. I've put out an alert, but they could be anywhere by now."

"What about Barb Rainer's place? Her farm is plenty big for them to be hiding out," said Emily.

"We searched. Deserted. Clothes pulled out of drawers, toothbrush gone. She left in a hurry."

"Then they got away with it?" said Emily. "That's it?"

"Of course not," said Ron. "We have the bus stations, airport, train station, highway—covered. And it's all over the news we're looking for them. We'll have them by morning."

Emily said, "Did you find out the victim's true identity?"

"Yeah," said Ron. "Paul Macintosh. He was a stock broker, then got into one of those pyramid schemes. Bunch of his clients lost their shirts."

"And he wasn't convicted?" asked Henry.

"He faked a suicide. Out in California. Left a suicide note, parked his car at the edge of a cliff overlooking the water, left his shoes and glasses in a neat little pile. Of course, the body was never recovered."

"Then what? He moved to Vermont?" asked Henry.

"Twelve years ago. Yeah."

"How did a stock broker manage to steal three identities?"

"He had a degree in information technology. Came in handy for stealing information."

"Thanks for the update," said Henry. He showed Ron out.

Emily put on a pot of coffee and heated up one of Maddy's pumpkin loaves. They gathered at the table for dessert and a game of Scrabble.

Henry said, "So much for a relaxing vacation."

"It was relaxing. We went fishing," said Mike. "In more ways than one. And I beat you at bowling."

"I had a great time," said Susan. "I bought some lovely things for my grandchildren, ate good food, and got to solve a puzzle."

"I wish you could stay longer," said Emily. "I wish you really were hunting for a retirement home here!"

There was a knock at the door. Emily said, "Rebecca left her laptop charger. I'll bet it's her." She opened the door. "You! What are you doing here?"

"I need your help." It was Barb Rainer. "The police are looking for me. They think I killed Chet."

"I know," said Emily.

Henry came up behind Emily and put his hands on her shoulders. "Don't let her in, she's a fugitive."

Emily said to Barb, "If you turn yourself in, you won't get hurt. Want me to call the detective for you? That's the only way I'm letting you in our house."

Henry said, "Wait there. I'll call right now."

"Not so fast," said Barb. She pulled a gun out of her pocket.

"Get on the couch, all of you." She held the gun to them and backed over to the door. Kirby and Patrice rushed in.

"What are you doing?" asked Susan. "There's no good way out of this. The three of you killed your mutual husband. If I found out my husband had two other wives, I'd probably do the same." Her heart pounded in her chest.

"We didn't mean to kill him. We just wanted to scare him. He came at me with the oar," said Patrice.

"How did he wind up in the boat in the first place?" asked Susan.

"I said I had a surprise for him. We were honeymooners, after all. I asked him to meet me in the woods and I'd show him. When he got there, I'd already tied the boat to the pier. I walked into the woods and met him in the car. I told him I had a moonlight boat ride planned for us. He fell for it, hook, line and sinker, so to speak."

"What happened when you got to the boat?" asked Henry.

Kirby said, "Barb picked me up at the inn. She and I hid under the pier. We were all going to confront him about what he did. I couldn't wait to see the look on his face when he saw all three of us and realized we knew."

"Barb and Kirby popped out of hiding," said Patrice. "He knew something was going on. He picked up the oar and went at me with it."

"I whacked him over the head with the other oar," said Kirby. He was trying to kill Patrice. I guess I hit him too hard. He fell into the water and we panicked."

"Why didn't you call for help?" asked Mike.

"We tried. I couldn't get a signal. Then, it started raining. Barb had parked by her family cabin at Fisherman's Cove. We were planning on taking him there to get it all out in the open. Instead, we left him in the water, got in the boat, and crossed the lake," said Patrice.

Barb said, "We had to do something with the boat. I knew the Amoses were gone for the winter and they'd given me a key in case of emergency. It was too heavy to drag. We dumped the motor. Then, we got the rest of the boat into their garage. Patrice didn't want to go back to the duplex without Blake. She thought her nosy landlady would be suspicious."

"So you let her into the Amos cabin," said Susan.

"They'll never know she was there," said Barb.

Susan said, "The wedding ring that was found on his body. It was from your wedding, Patrice?"

"Yeah. God knows how he kept track of the rotation."

Henry said, "How did you find out about each other?"

Barb said, "Patrice and I live in the same town, for God's sake. If he hadn't gotten so bold, maybe his secret would be safe. I saw his car parked in front of Il Trattoria's Ristorante. I waited until he came out. With a woman. With Patrice."

Patrice said, "She followed the car back to my duplex."

Barb said, "I did some checking and found out he wasn't a forest ranger. How could I have been so stupid, believing him all those years? Anyway, the next morning, I went back to the duplex, waited for him to leave, then knocked on Patrice's door. We compared notes and realized we were married to the same man."

Patrice said, "After comparing notes, Barb and I realized there were periods of days that were unaccounted for. I hired a private investigator and found out about Kirby."

"I was furious at him," said Kirby. "I'd just found out I was pregnant. I wanted to kill him. Not literally, at that point. We came up with this plan to make him face the music and tell us the truth about who he was. I drove up here and we put it together."

"You should have called the police right away," said Susan. "It was an accident. You can't get out of this. The police are looking for all three of you."

"That's where you come in," said Barb. "Henry, you're gonna drive us to the Canadian border. Your wife and friends will be locked in my barn. The police already searched my property, they won't go back again. When the three of us are safely over the border, I'll give Henry the key. He'll come back and release you." Barb looked around the room. She picked up Mike's Yankees cap from the coffee table. "Phone's in here. Now."

They slowly tossed their phones into the cap. Susan hoped the cloud had stored all her family photos, especially the ones of her granddaughters and the ultrasound picture of the new baby.

Barb continued. "Stand up. All of you. Walk toward the door with your hands on your heads. Now." She pointed the gun at Emily's head. They shuffled toward the door. "Grab your keys, Henry."

Henry said, "I'll have to get them from the kitchen."

"Go on. Hurry. No funny business. Get your wife's car keys also."

Henry went into the kitchen and weighed his options. He could make a run for it out the back door, but they might shoot Emily when they discovered he left. He could grab a kitchen knife and use it as a weapon. He could crash the Jeep on the way out of town, but it was iffy. If he were knocked unconscious, he might not get the key to the barn.

"Hurry up in there!" yelled Barb. She took Emily's keys off the hall table.

Henry grabbed a steak knife and hid it under his jacket. "Coming." Thank God Maddy was spending the night at her friend's house. They crowded into Henry's Jeep. Susan felt her chest tighten and she grasped Mike's hand.

Barb tossed Emily's keys to Patrice. "You drive the Audi. We'll meet back at my place."

They pulled out of the driveway and around the lake. Susan felt like she was about to vomit. Emily squirmed next to Mike. She felt under the seat with her feet, hoping she could take Barb by surprise by jolting the passenger seat forward.

When they came to a stoplight, Susan tried to open the door and make a run for it. She carefully grabbed the handle, then pushed. The door didn't budge. *Barb must have turned on the child safety lock.*

"Turn left at the light," said Barb. They were nearing her farm. The road would become isolated in a few minutes. Susan remembered from their visit during the daytime what a lonely stretch of road lay ahead and now it was dark. No one would cross their path.

Susan gave it one last try. "Why don't you leave us out here and drive both cars to Canada? By the time someone finds us, you'll be over the border."

Emily said, "We're miles from town and it's hours before daylight. If I were you, I wouldn't waste the time locking us up. Let us out. Right here on the side of the road. Hurry before the police catch up to you."

"They won't be looking for my car," said Henry. "Or Emily's. It's a good plan."

Police sirens blared. Susan prayed they were coming for them. She squeezed Mike's hand. Red lights throbbed in the rearview mirror. A cruiser screeched to a stop in front of Henry's car. Two officers stormed the car.

"Get out with your hands up."

Susan felt like she could finally breathe. The officer slapped handcuffs on Barb.

Henry said, "There are two more. They're driving an Audi."

"Already got them," said the officer.

Ron Wooster came over. "Everybody okay?"

Henry said, "Glad you got here when you did. How did you know what was going on?"

"Your daughter," said Ron. "Maddy's sleepover was canceled. She was in her room the whole time. She heard everything and called us." Maddy, who had been in Ron's car, ran over and hugged Henry and Emily.

Emily said, "You just saved our lives. Who knows what would have happened had we been taken to that isolated barn."

"I'm glad you're both okay," said Maddy.

Susan said, "Quite a daughter you've got there."

"Yes, she is," said Emily. "This is just the beginning. When she becomes a vet, there's no telling how much good she'll do in this world."

Henry said, "Let's go home. It's Susan and Mike's last night here. I wonder if they'll want to come back after tonight."

"Of course we will," said Susan. "Nothing like new adventures with old friends."

"To new adventures," said Mike. "Emily, I've got an important question to ask."

"What is it?" said Emily

"Is there any more of that pumpkin bread at the house?"

The End

# About the Author

Award winning author Diane Weiner is a veteran public school teacher and mother of four grown children. Fond memories of reading mysteries by Nancy Drew and Mary Higgins Clark on snowy weekends in upstate New York inspired her to write books that would bring that kind of joy to others. Being an animal lover, she is a vegetarian and shares her home with two precious cats—Chelsea and Callie. In her free time, she enjoys running, shopping, attending theater productions, and spending time with her family.

Visit **dianeweinerauthor.com** to find out more about the author.

Made in the USA
Middletown, DE
11 May 2022

65618118R00059